The Story of Oog

Or, A New Thinker's Guide to the Forest

by

LEN VLAHOS

ALSO BY

The Scar Boys

Scar Girl

Life in a Fishbowl

Hard Wired

Girl on the Ferris Wheel (with Julie Halpern)

Serge & Roscoe

DEDICATIONS

LEN VLAHOS

For Kristen... You have supported each of my books in every way possible, and now you're publishing them??
This wouldn't exist with you. Neither would I.

RICHARD DiSTEFANO

With love to Alex and Lindsey: I'm proud to be your dad.
And also with love to Diane: I'm so lucky to have met you.

First published in the United States of America, November 2025 by Left Field Publishing.

ISBN: 9781966883005 (paperback)
ISBN: 9781966883012 (ebook)
ISBN: 9781966883029 (audiobook)

Library of Congress Control Number: 2025918901

Book Cover by Kristen Gilligan
Printed in the United States of America

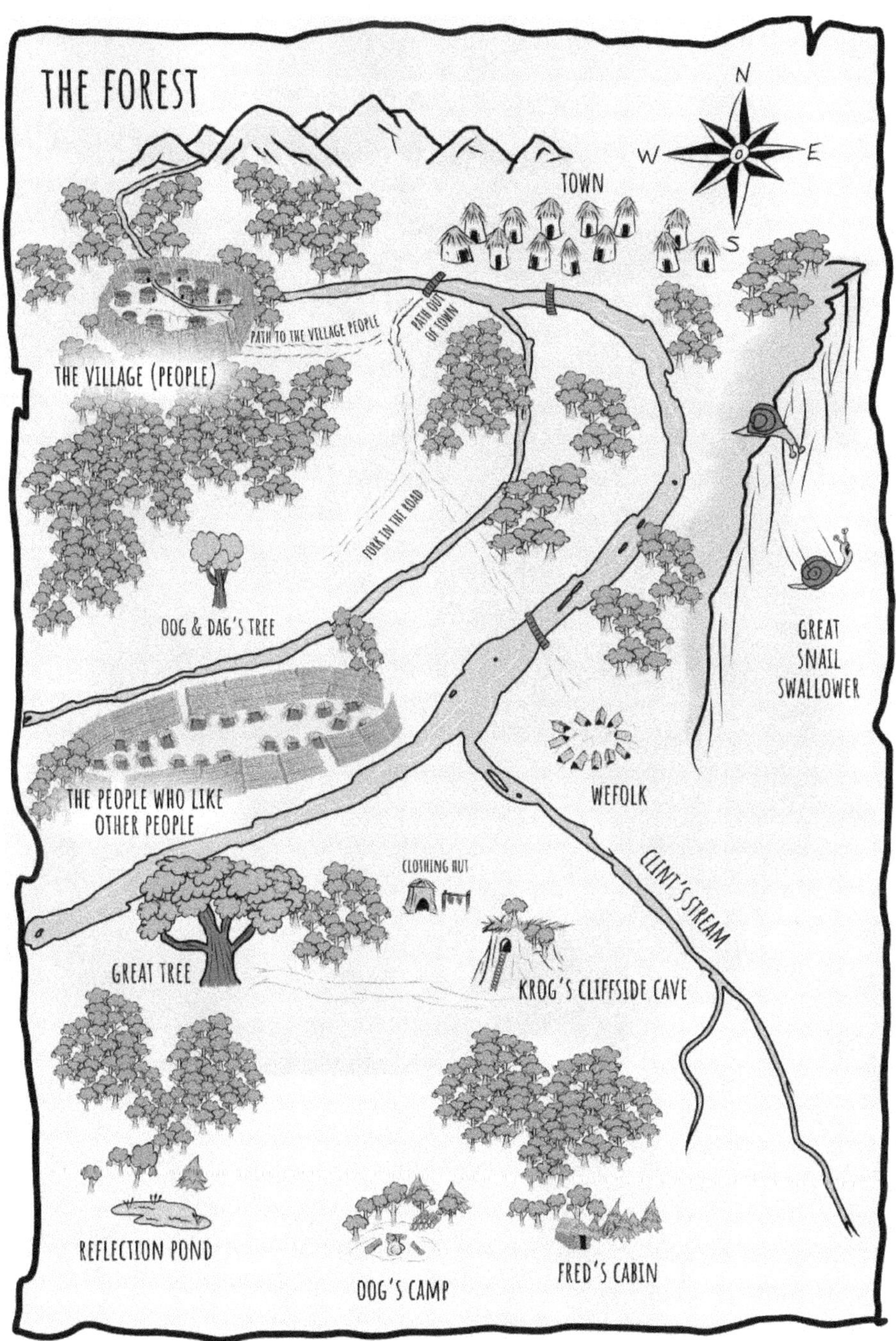
THE FOREST
N
W
E
S
TOWN
PATH TO THE VILLAGE PEOPLE
PATH OUT OF TOWN
THE VILLAGE (PEOPLE)
FORK IN THE ROAD
OOG & DAG'S TREE
GREAT SNAIL SWALLOWER
WEFOLK
THE PEOPLE WHO LIKE OTHER PEOPLE
CLOTHING HUT
CLINT'S STREAM
GREAT TREE
KROG'S CLIFFSIDE CAVE
REFLECTION POND
OOG'S CAMP
FRED'S CABIN

1.

Once upon a time, there was a boy.

He was walking through the Forest one day, scratching himself, like he always did.

Drooling, like he always did.

Smelling the air for food, like he always did.

On this particular day, as the boy was passing a small pond, he noticed something strange. He looked down and saw another boy looking back at him. When he bent down to touch the other boy's face, the water rippled, and the face disappeared.

The boy had never seen a reflection before. Or rather, he had never known he had seen a reflection before. He did not know what a reflection, or even a face, was, because until this day, he had not had a single thought.

At all.

Ever.

The boy thought to himself, *Who was that good looking fellow with the protruding forehead, and where did he go?* Then, he paused. *Hey,* he thought, *that was me!*

But wait. What does that mean? What is me? Who am I? Am I thinking? Holy crap! I think I'm thinking!

Excited by his newfound power of thought, he needed to tell

someone. He moved quickly through the Forest looking for other people, and when he came upon a group in a clearing—they were scratching themselves, drooling, and smelling the air for food—he started waving his arms and shouting.

"I can think! I am conscious!" he yelled with joy. But what came out of his mouth was "Oog agergo grooggo! Oog egaw ofoosgoos!" Because the boy had only just begun to think, he could not yet make words.

The people were confused.

They were terrified.

They picked up sticks.

They picked up dirt.

They picked up rocks.

They hurled their sticks and dirt and rocks at the boy, chasing him from that part of the Forest.

Bewildered and frightened, the boy fled. He ducked under and around fallen trees and large boulders. He ran across and along streams. He trampled up and down hills, through clearings, and into the deepest, darkest part of the wood.

He ran.

And ran.

And ran some more.

The boy ran for hours until he found himself in a part of the Forest that was entirely unfamiliar. He sat down on the ground and started to cry.

He cried.

And cried.

And cried some more.

The boy did not know he was crying, as he had never before cried.

He only knew that his face was leaking and he could not stop it from happening. And while it made him feel worse, it made him feel better, too.

Finally, the boy fell asleep.

2.

When the boy woke, it was dark.

But it was not entirely dark.

There was a flickering light nearby.

The light was coming from a fire.

Huddled around the fire was a group of older people, all of them staring at the boy.

The boy had never contemplated age before because, until this day, he had never contemplated anything. But in the glow of the dancing flames he could see the skin of these people was rough, their bodies bent forward, their hair white or in some cases patchy and missing. He felt his own skin; it was smooth. He looked at the hair on his arms; it was dark brown.

I must be young, he thought, *but how young?*

He shook his head to clear his thoughts and noticed how close to the fire these people were sitting.

The boy had only seen fire once before. A large spear of death had shot from the sky and split a tree in two, engulfing it in flames. He was much smaller when this happened, and he had stared at the fire in wonder. He was so enthralled he didn't notice the flames start to eat the forest around him until a bigger person had grabbed him by the hair and dragged him to safety. Once his rescuer had moved them a reasonable distance from the fire, she went back to scratching herself, drooling, and smelling the air for food. But the boy had continued to watch the fire until the water falling from the sky vanquished it. Perhaps, he considered now, I was starting to think even then.

Again, he shook his head. All this thinking was proving to be a distraction.

These older people were too close to the fire, and they were in danger.

He stood and marched toward them with purpose. "Run, you fools, run! That fire will eat you!" What came out of his mouth was "Grooodo, googos, grooodo! Dokn sadokoooo gogogodoso!"

One of the oldest people, the man closest to the fire, looked at the hysterical boy for a moment, stood up, and then bonked him on the head with a big stick.

The boy hit the ground like a dead bird falling from a tree, and was, once again, unconscious.

NOTES ON THINKING

Many millennia after the boy and the old people had lived, a seventeen-year-old French boy stands up. It is his first time at the meeting of the Philosophers Union.

"Allo, everyone, my name is René."

"Allo, René," the hundred or so grown men reply in unison.

"Okay, here we go. I think..." he begins, pausing for effect, letting his voice rise at the end of the second word, teasing his audience, not showing a hint of the butterflies in his stomach.

"Oooh," someone says, "a showman!"

"'I think,'" says another. "Nice beginning."

"I think," René starts again, "theeeerefoooore..." He emphasizes each syllable of this new word and pauses longer, a devilish smile playing at the corner of his mouth.

"'Therefore!' Brilliant!" shouts an older man in the front row.

"Is there more?" another person asks. "Please tell us there's more!"

"Oui, oui," says René, beaming at how well he's doing. "Wait for it..." he teases again.

"Tell us!" someone shouts, nearly apoplectic.

"I think," René says, "therefore... I...am...smart!"

The room is deathly quiet.

"You think, therefore you're...smart?" a man near the back asks.

"Oui. Very good, don't you think?" René having expected applause when he rose to speak, absent-mindedly stroked his pencil thin mustache, a nervous tick he had developed in recent months; the stress of philosophizing was really taking a toll on the young man.

"I don't know," the same man responds. "François thinks all the time, and he's an idiot."

"Hey!" François objects. The audience laughs.

"Maybe it needs to be shorter," a tall thin man with a high thin voice offers.

"Shorter?" René, asks, his anxiety growing. "How?"

"Oh, I don't know, maybe just, 'I am smart!'" This draws mild applause.

"But what if he's not smart?" François offers. Again, laughter. "Hey!"

"What about," someone else suggests, "just, 'Therefore I am!'"

"No, no. If we use therefore, there must be something before it," a new voice offers.

René, concerned about the use of the word 'we,' tries to wrestle back control of the room. "How about...?" He pauses, thinking quickly. "I eat; therefore I am smart."

Silence.

"I think maybe it's the word smart that's bothering me," the tall thin man offers. "How about 'I eat food, therefore I am.'"

"Now we're getting somewhere," a person from the back interjects.

"No," René says, exasperated, "we're not. What does food have to do with any of this?"

"I don't know, you brought it up."

René blushes, realizing he did.

"Now that you mention it," a short round man in the second row cuts in, "I'm pretty hungry. Is there anything to eat here?"

With that, there are murmurs of agreement and the assembly breaks to forage for food.

"Great," René says to no one in particular. "Just great."

Though René, whose last name is Descartes, will eventually get his maxim right, on this day he is crestfallen. Thinking, and thinking about thinking, it turns out, is hard work.

René's ancestor, the boy who is the hero of our story, a cousin four hundred and sixty times removed, was still figuring out what to think of these older people, and how best to use his newfound powers of thought.

3.

The boy woke several minutes later to find the same old man watching him. Angry that he had been bonked on the head—another feeling that did not require the power of thought, for what creature is not angry when bonked on the head?—the boy started to growl.

"Quiet, my young friend," the old man said. "There is no danger here." And what came out of the old man's mouth was: "Quiet, my young friend. There is no danger here."

The boy did not understand the words, but he could sense they were meant to comfort him.

He stopped growling.

He sat up.

He blinked.

The other old people sat in small groups around the fire. They talked in hushed tones, stealing occasional glances at the boy. Some held hands, some picked bugs out of each other's hair.

"Come," the old man said. He patted the log on which he was seated. Next to the log was the big stick he had used to bonk the boy on the head. The boy looked from the man to the stick to the fire. The old man noticed this and smiled.

"I am sorry for hitting you on the head, but you seemed quite out of your mind."

While he did not understand a word of this, the soothing tone of the man's voice gave the boy confidence.

"Oogogo godro goog?" he asked.

"You have gone through the Change, haven't you, my young friend?" the old man said. "You see things now."

Again, the boy did not understand the words, but again, they were soothing. And this time he had the feeling they were connected to his newfound powers of thought. He didn't know why, but he felt sure of it.

"Come, sit," the old man said, patting his log again.

Repositioning himself from sitting to squatting, the boy crab-walked a few feet closer to the log. He looked sidelong at the fire and sat back down on the dirt.

The old man stared at the boy and understood. "Ah yes, you are frightened by the fire. But see?" the old man said, pointing at the flames. "They bring warmth." He held his hands toward the fire, palms out, and sighed with relief. Then he got up, moved a few feet away, wrapped his arms around his body, and shivered.

The boy understood! The fire brings warmth! He nodded and continued his crabwalk to the log but was still unable to completely overcome his fear. He hunched on the ground at the end of the log, eyeing the fire with suspicion.

The old man nodded, touched his own chest, and said, "Groog. My name is Groog."

The boy thought very hard about this. Why would this man touch his chest and say this word? Aha! he thought. His chest is called Groog!

"Groog," the boy repeated slowly.

"Yes, excellent! Groog!"

Then Groog pointed at the boy.

The boy pointed at Groog.

"No, no, no," Groog answered, and he pointed again at the boy. "What is your name?" The old man once again touched his chest and said, "Groog." Then, he pointed at the boy's chest.

This time the boy understood. Because, remember, he could now think.

With great pride the boy touched his own chest and said, "Groog!"

The old man laughed. "No," he said, "no." Now he touched his head, his arms, his chest, his legs, and his feet. "Groog," he said firmly.

The boy puzzled over this. Were all the parts of the old man's body called the same thing? That would get confusing. 'Hey, there's a spider on your Groog,' would not be especially helpful if everything was called Groog.

The boy, feeling flustered, looked at the old man, who, for his part, sat waiting patiently. After a moment, he again touched his chest, his palm splayed flat, and said, "Groog."

"Oh, for crying out loud," said one of the other people around the fire, "his name is Groog!"

Groog put a finger to his lips to silence his friend, but the interruption gave him an idea. He touched his chest and said, "Groog." He then pointed at the person who had spoken and said, "Grag." He pointed at another and said, "Moog." He pointed from person to person, giving each a new word.

And then the boy understood.

He rose to his feet.

He clapped his hands.

He smiled in delight.

The boy pointed at the old man and said, “Groog!”

“Yes,” Groog said, “my name is Groog.” He stood up, too, and he and the boy hugged in celebration.

“Oh brah-vo,” muttered Grag.

They sat back down, Groog on the log by the fire, the boy a few feet away. Now Groog pointed at the boy. “What is your name?”

This time the boy understood the question but did not know the answer. The only sound he ever seemed to make with any consistency was Oog, so he said that.

“Oog.”

“Welcome, Oog, welcome.”

Oog did not understand, but he sensed the words were good.

They gave him comfort.

They gave him peace.

Tired from his long day, from his running, and his crying, and his thinking, and his being bonked on the head, Oog laid down at Groog's feet and went to sleep.

And he slept.

And he slept.

And he slept some more.

4.

The waxing and waning of nearly two dozen moons passed while Oog stayed with Groog and the other old people.

Oog learned many useful things:

He learned to sharpen sticks for killing food.

He learned how to trap animals.

He learned to tell the seasons from the passing of the stars.

But there were two things Oog learned that towered above all others. First, he learned language.

He started slowly: a noun here ("head"), a verb there ("bonk"). Groog taught him that the leader of the village was called "Mother," and that fire was called "fire." Oog's sentences grew more complex and sophisticated. He went from "Oog hungry" to "Do we have anything to eat. I'm famished" in the course of a few months. He also learned that Groog referred to the collected group of old people as, simply, the People.

The second important thing Oog learned was how to tend the fire. He was shown which sticks burned the best and longest, and where to forage for them; he learned that fire eats air; and he was schooled in the myriad ways of protecting the fire from the seemingly ceaseless rain that fell in this part of the Forest.

During a particularly heavy rain, Oog watched as Groog pulled a thin, braided vine (Oog learned this was called a "rope") tied in an intricate pattern around five trees that surrounded the fire pit. "We chose this spot for the fire because of the arrangement of these trees," Groog said as he pulled the rope taut. As he did, a large covering made from the skins of deer, fox, and other animals, rose from the ground and spread between the trees, forming a kind of roof over the fire, keeping the rain off.

Oog was beside himself with joy as he watched this. He examined every inch of the contraption until he thought he understood how it worked. "This is incredible," he said to Groog. "Did you make this?"

A broad smile played across Groog's face as he nodded.

"What is the purpose of this?" Oog asked, pulling on a small stick that supported one strand of the rope.

"No, wait!" Groog exclaimed. But it was too late.

The tarp collapsed and fell onto the fire, smothering it. Large billows of smoke poured out from the edges of the tarp, filling the Forest with a thick, acrid fog, stinging Oog's eyes and making it hard to breathe.

"Help!" Groog wailed, and the People sprang to action.

Grag was first on the scene. He, with the help of others, pulled the tarp back while Groog, who had let go of his rope, added fuel to the fire. He looked at Oog pleadingly and Oog started adding fuel to the fire, too.

As soon as Groog was satisfied the fire would not go out, he repaired the damage to the tarp contraption and raised the roof one more time, all of the People chanting, "Raise the roof, raise the roof," as he did.

Once the crisis was averted, Oog, wracked with guilt, sat down heavily and began to cry. He was finding there was a correlation between how much one thought and how much one cried.

Groog, his hands and face covered with soot, sat down next to him.

"It is okay, my young friend," he said, patting Oog on the back with a gentleness that filled Oog with a kind of warmth that outshone even the warmth of the fire.

"No," said Grag, "it is not okay. In fact, his blunder calls for a new word." Those nearby looked up in surprise.

"And what would be the use for this word?" Groog asked.

"To describe a bumbler, one who is prone to wreaking havoc."

"Does the word bumbler not serve that purpose?"

"No, it is too...soft."

Both Groog and Grag looked to Mother who sat nearby. She was staring sternly, though not unkindly, at Oog. She shifted her gaze to Grag and Groog. "It is Grag's right. We will have a council of words this evening."

That night the People talked long with much laughter and told many stories. There were many ideas proposed to describe the particular kind of bumbling of which Oog had been guilty: a doctorsmith, an alvin, a peregrine. In the end, the group settled on the word "gilligan." Oog was a gilligan. He took it in stride and laughed along with the rest.

As the council and evening drew to a close, Oog huddled close to the fire trying to get the chill out of his bones. "Why," he asked during a lull in the conversation, "do we have a roof only over the fire? Why do we not have roofs over the places we sit, sleep, and think?"

The entire group went silent as each person stared at Oog in astonishment. The next day a project was begun—the largest public works project in recent memory—to build more roofs. And the next night, another word council was held. At its conclusion, it was determined that Oog was both a "gilligan" and a "genius."

He liked the sound of that very much.

5.

Oog and Groog were sitting on the log tending the fire, stoking hot coals, and adding wood from a nearby pile. They had been quiet for a few moments, each lost in his own thoughts. Oog loved to lose himself in his thoughts. For all the questions he had already asked Groog, many more careened through his mind. They fascinated him, thrilled him, and sometimes frightened him.

Oog wondered what made the questions in the first place. Was there something inside his head? He had once seen inside the head of a wild boar as it was being prepared for cooking. The sight was disgusting—squishy, gray, and soaked in blood. But then boars couldn't think; what was inside his head had to be different. He imagined ropes and pulleys, like the ones that kept the tarp over the fire when it rained. Thinking about thinking led him to thinking about everything else.

"What makes...all of this?" Oog asked Groog, gesturing at the fire, the trees, the People. "Is it magic?"

Groog lifted one eyebrow (something Oog had tried to imitate many times without success), and his mouth looked as if he were sucking on something sour. "Magic?"

Earlier that same day, Oog had been introduced to the concept of magic by one of the People, a woman named Skag. She had shown Oog a small pebble; it was worn smooth and about the size of the fingernail on Oog's pinky. Skag held it loosely in the palm of her left hand.

"It is a pebble," Oog had said with confidence. He was still new enough at thinking and speaking that he felt a small swell of pride in knowing the answer to Skag's unasked question.

"Yes, yes," she said, "I know it's a pebble. Look at it carefully."

Oog did. He bent so low his nose was almost touching the small stone lying in Skag's palm.

"Not that carefully," she said. There was an edge to Skag's voice, which didn't surprise Oog, as Skag and Grag were mates. Oog stood up straighter.

"Now watch." With an even, easy movement, Skag passed her right hand over the hand with the stone. When her left palm was revealed again, the stone was gone. Then she held up both hands to show they were empty. Oog looked on the ground, but the stone was nowhere to be seen.

Oog's gut reaction was fear. He might have turned and ran were Skag not smiling so broadly.

"Where did it go?" Oog asked. His voice was soft and strained at the same time.

"It's in your ear."

"What?" Oog's hands, now terrified extensions of his terrified body, shot up to his ears feeling for the stone, but other than coarse hair, there was nothing there.

"No, it's not."

"Yes, it is."

He felt again. "No, it's not."

"Yes, it is." This time Skag reached out toward Oog's ear and pulled her hand back with the pebble held between her thumb and forefinger.

Oog yelped, his hands going again to his ears, fearful that more pebbles might start tumbling out. "How did you do that?"

"Magic," Skag had said, and wandered away laughing.

Oog stayed rooted to the spot. "Magic," he said out loud, letting the new word roll around his tongue. "Magic," he said again.

Now, seated on the log, Oog looked expectantly at Groog. "Yes, magic," he said in answer to his friend's question.

"Did Skag pull a stone from your nose?" Groog asked, an annoyed smile playing at the corner of his mouth.

"My ear."

"Ah," Groog said. "That is not magic. It is a trick."

"A trick?"

"A way of fooling thinkers for enjoyment." This confused Oog terribly. He was about to protest when Groog held up a hand. "She hides the pebble in her hand in a way you do not notice. It's very clever, but it is not magic. There is no magic."

"No magic?" asked Oog. "But what about all the things we cannot explain? Why is fire, fire? Why are trees, trees? Why—?"

Groog laid a hand on Oog's shoulder to stop him. "We call it Nature."

"But what is Nature?"

"Nature," said Groog, thinking for a moment, "is everything. The Forest, the birds, you, me, the wind; it is all Nature."

Oog thought on this for a long time. It was good to have

explanations for things. While he did not really understand what Nature was, Oog was happy to have a way in which he could think about the world.

"So," he began. "I am Nature?"

"Yes," said Groog.

"And you are Nature?"

"Yes."

"And that stick you used to bonk me on the head the first night we met? That was Nature, too?"

Groog laughed. It was a pleasing sound, Oog thought, like a strong wind through the leaves. "Yes. Everything we can see, smell, hear, taste, and touch, is part of Nature."

Oog, very excited at this discovery, clapped his hands together once. "Brilliant!" He thought for a moment, wondering what other things he could explain with Nature.

Then he thought of death.

Before he went through the Change, before he could think, Oog had encountered death in the Forest many times. Dead animals, dead trees, even dead people. It had never fazed him. How could it? He couldn't think. But since becoming self-aware, the idea of death terrified him. What if he died? Dead things didn't appear to think. Nor did they walk or talk or smile or laugh or have their eyes leak. They experienced no happiness, no sadness, no anger, no love. There was no way to rationalize death, so every time the thought had popped into his mind prior to this day, Oog had shoved it away. Of course, it was the unanswered questions that bothered Oog the most, like an itch inside his head that absolutely had to be scratched.

"So, when we die," he asked Groog in a voice that was barely a whisper, "we are still a part of Nature?"

"Yes. Death is part of Nature, too."

"So, if we are Nature, when we die, what happens to us?"

Groog looked at his protégé for a long moment and then said, "Well, nothing happens. We just die. Life ends."

Oog stared, perplexed. The answer was unsatisfying. "Who made Nature?"

"No one made Nature. It has always been and shall always be."

"How do you know?"

"I believe what my eyes show me."

"I don't understand."

Groog started to explain, stopped, and started again. "You asked once why rain doesn't fall up."

"Yes."

"You didn't ask if rain did fall up."

"No."

"Why?"

"Because I have never seen rain fall up."

"Exactly," Groog said, clapping Oog on the back and beaming.

"But does that mean it cannot fall up?"

"Good question." Oog liked it when Groog complimented his questions. "It is possible for rain to fall up. But until it does, I have no reason, based on what I have seen and experienced, to believe it ever will. Do you know Glig?"

Oog did know Glig. She was the quietest of all the People. She radiated a sadness that made Oog want to both help and shun her.

"Her mate died many seasons ago; his name was Occam."

"That's a curious name."

"Eh," Groog shrugged. "Anyway, Occam liked to say that the

simplest explanation for things was usually the right explanation. Nature is a much simpler explanation for the world than is magic."

Oog was still unsatisfied. Groog's explanation took meaning and purpose out of life in a way that left Oog feeling empty. He was about to protest when Groog laid a hand on his young friend's shoulder.

"Come," he said, "it's time for the Stories."

Oog took more delight in the Stories than in almost any other activity in the community of the People. Once every few days, the People would sit around the fire and recount their history. They would correct one another, argue over minutiae, embellish events (or so Oog presumed), and laugh. It was the laughter Oog liked best, and he would often find himself joining in.

The Stories seemed to fuel his imagination the way giant logs fueled the fire, and they seemed to make him smarter. Oog paid close attention on this night as Mother retold the story of how these people became the People.

Mother was the first to think, she explained. Much as had happened to Oog, she awoke one day when she was young and saw the world differently. Groog was next, then Grag, then each of the others in turn. They had all lived in the same part of the Forest and had gravitated toward one another.

Early in their communal existence, when they still didn't do much beyond scratching themselves, drooling, and smelling the air for food—though they did notice they were drooling decidedly less—the sky darkened, the wind picked up, and a great storm sprang from nowhere. The (not yet old) People were huddled together under the trees for safety and warmth when one of the trees was struck by a spear of light from the sky. Oog wondered if it was the same spear of light he had seen as a young boy.

When the tree split and caught fire, several of the People were burned and died. Others ran in fear. But not Groog. He turned, faced the fire, and felt its warmth. It felt good. It beat back the cold and damp of the storm. Seeing the tree burn, Groog found other pieces of wood to feed the fire. Mother saw this and helped him. Slowly, others came back and helped as well. The fire had been burning without rest—over the many, many revolutions of the stars—since that night.

"But if the fire goes out, can you not make more fire?" Oog asked.

"No," Groog answered. "We have tried many things—throwing sharpened sticks at the clouds, yelling with one voice at the sky, banging logs together—but none have worked. Only the sky can make fire."

These all seemed to be good and wise approaches to try to make fire, thought Oog, but he was convinced there must be a way. He suspected the others would think him foolish, or worse, arrogant, were he to say this out loud, so he kept the idea to himself.

"Life was good," Mother continued. "We learned to forage for food and hunt together."

"Not Grag," someone interjected. "The last time he tried to hunt, he speared Gorg in the ass." There was raucous laughter now. Even Grag had trouble tamping down the smirk trying to burst forth upon his face.

"We learned all we could about Nature," Groog said, emphasizing the word and staring at Oog. "We tended to those who got sick, wept for those who died, and through it all, the fire kept us warm and safe."

There were nods of assent and murmurs of agreement.

“The fire,” Mother said, “must never go out.”

Everyone repeated the phrase in unison. “The fire must never go out.”

“Never,” added Groog, and everyone repeated that, too.

NOTES ON DEATH

Homo sapiens—the species that long ago included Oog, Groog, and everyone else you will meet in this story—have made an art form of personifying inanimate objects and abstract concepts. They have written books in which brain tumors, violence, and crack cocaine are characters. They have built myriad machines to talk to and instruct them. They even erected a large city in the swamps of North America devoted to the worship of an annoying cartoon mouse with a falsetto voice who wears pants and shoes, but no shirt. (Perhaps, anthropologists will posit, the mouse dresses this way to mirror the fashion choices made by many of the human inhabitants in the cities that surround the swamp.)

Chief among the things humans like to anthropomorphize is the concept of death: The Grim Reaper, the boogey man, devils and demons, are all meant to help humans make sense of the senselessness of death. As if by giving death a face and a voice, they might find a way to reason with it. Many of their stories feature heroes conquering a personified death.

But those were only stories. Death, Homo sapiens will learn (too late) always wins in the end. (Now, how's that for some foreshadowing?)

6.

The first time He with No Name had a thought, it terrified him. Until that time, he had wandered through the Forest drooling, scratching, and sniffing, just like everyone else.

Then, one day, he looked down and saw another person, an older person, lying on the ground. He nudged the lying-down person with his foot, but the lying-down person did not stir. He tried again, this time harder, but still there was no response. Finally, he got down on his knees and yelled into the lying-down person's ears. Nothing.

He with No Name sat back on his haunches and stared at the person. It was a man, and he looked frozen in a moment of anguish.

No Name sniffed the air; a scent of decay was on the wind. But there was another scent, too.

Sorrow.

The odor was not anything he had smelled before, like a strange blend of rotting tree trunks, thimbleweed, and animal droppings. And what was more, it was not something he could see.

This recognition of sorrow was, No Name realized, his first thought.

His next thought, much less abstract, was that the lying-down person was dead.

Very dead.

Unequivocally and not-very-likely-to-ever-be-anything-again-other-than-dead, dead.

This brought terror into No Name's heart. He did not know why, he only knew he did not want to be dead himself. He scrambled away and hid behind a tree. From there, he stared at the formerly just lying-down and now lying-down-and-very-dead person.

No Name had seen dead things in the Forest—squirrels, foxes, birds—and none of them had ever done anything even remotely interesting. Before today, he hadn't given dead things, or other things for that matter, any thought. But now, No Name's world had changed. He knew the dead person was dead, and knowing made all the difference.

No Name did not like thinking. He did not like it at all. He envied the non-thinkers. Ignorance, he said to himself, is bliss. Or he would have, had ignorance or bliss been concepts he could grasp. What he actually said to himself was "Gofogofoo." He would not have been able to define this new word if asked, though he knew it meant something along the lines of "I wish I didn't know that."

No matter how hard he tried, No Name could not stop thinking. All that day and for the several days that followed, No Name would run each time a new thought popped into his head.

Why does the rain make dirt into mud?

"Gofogofoo," he'd say, and he would run, trying to get away from the thought.

Why do some cavepeople have chest bumps and I do not?

"Gofogofoo." He would take off again.

Who am I? Why am I here? Why do I smell so bad?

"Gofogofoo." "Gofogofoo." "Gofogofoo." He would run, run, and run some more.

Each time he caught himself thinking, no matter the thought, off he would go. When he became so winded he could go no farther, No Name would collapse on the ground, the thought, whatever it had been, driven from his brain. But no sooner would his breath return than a new thought would pop into his mind. Lying on the forest floor, staring at the long branches of the trees, he would think, *Why do acorns fall faster than leaves?* And away he went.

After a week of this thinking and running, with occasional breaks to eat and sleep, No Name had a new thought: I am exhausted.

Then, he had yet another, more purposeful thought: *I cannot help but think.*

This more purposeful thought careened through every corner of his mind, trying to find something to refute it, but it was no use. This was, No Name realized, an incontrovertible truth. He was now a thinker.

He tried to convey his newfound powers of thought to each person he encountered, but the response was never satisfying. They either shuffled farther away from him—to do their drooling, scratching, and sniffing out of harm's way—or they chased him, throwing sticks and dirt and rocks.

No Name remained utterly alone. It was at times terrifying, at other times anxiety-inducing, and almost never happy.

One day, as No Name wandered through the Forest contemplating his predicament, he happened on a spiderweb. It was a large, ornate, and complicated structure that stretched several feet between two trees. While No Name had seen spider webs before, he had never seen one like this. As he watched, one unsuspecting insect after another—flies, beetles, even a wasp—found themselves trapped in the web. Each struggled, and with the exception of the wasp, which beat its wings with a fury that No Name found fascinating, none escaped.

No Name watched for hours and hours, until eventually, the spider came to feed.

NOTES ON PROBABILITY

More generations after the age of Oog than a person would bother to count, a very clever but very gloomy man named John Graunt used mathematics and public records to discern the likelihood a person would die before their next birthday. He published this information in something he called an "actuarial table." When questioned on the name of his thoroughly depressing invention, Graunt is purported to have said, "I was going for something that sounded really sexy."

Had the kind of math used by Graunt existed in the time of Oog, it could have been extrapolated to show that, with more than ten thousand humans in the Forest, and with roughly half of them being older than sixteen, and roughly half of these being thinkers, it was extremely improbable that No Name had failed to encounter other thinkers to this point in his life.

Another branch of science called physics noted that the improbable is very much possible. And one infamous scientist, a man named Murphy, noted that the improbable, when it will result in something especially bad happening, will always come to pass. Murphy died when he tossed a small ball in the air, the ball hitting an apple, the apple falling to the ground and hitting a stone, the stone leaping up and hitting Murphy in the knee, and Murphy falling backwards and hitting his head on a boulder, where he lost consciousness and bled out. (All this was witnessed by a young boy named Goldberg, who found it morbidly fascinating.)

This is a long way of saying that improbable though it was, No Name had not encountered a single thinker in more than two revolutions of the stars, and the loneliness and isolation were starting to warp his brain.

7.

After watching the spider lure prey into its web, No Name devised a way of luring people into a different kind of web. He didn't want to eat them the way the spider ate flies and beetles; he wanted to use them for his own gain. He made his quarry comfortable, fed them, and provided a safe and happy environment. He would reward each of his charges with extra food or a pat on the shoulder when they did something well. No Name did this for weeks, until those he had drawn close became reliant on him for their most basic needs.

Then began the beatings.

Wander away when No Name needed something? A beating. Steal food from another member of their little community? A beating. Defecate near where they slept? An especially harsh beating.

Through this system of carrots and sticks—well, actually squirrel meat and sticks—No Name amassed a cadre of non-thinkers who would do his bidding. They hunted for No Name, they picked nits from No Name's hair, and they recruited more non-thinkers to No Name's army. The more an individual non-thinker gained No Name's favor, the more he rewarded them. The more they fell out of favor, the more he punished them.

Over time, No Name's captives evolved into a rugged band of

marauding thugs. They would take food from other non-thinkers, sometimes pummeling them in the process. They would kill animals indiscriminately, usually just to satisfy No Name's bloodlust. They would even fight each other just to gain favor with their leader.

As No Name's power over this army of non-thinkers grew, his conscience, which had never really developed in the first place, shrank; first to the size of an acorn, then to a small stone, then to a grain of sand. But No Name knew nothing of this. It takes a conscience larger than a grain of sand to realize to what depths power can corrupt a soul.

No Name ruled this band of high-functioning monkeys as a kind of mad tyrant. If one of them wandered off in the night, No Name would lead the others on a hunt, killing the escapee on sight.

Fear was their master.

As more and more non-thinkers were recruited, No Name's territory increased.

And then, one day, on the far-flung edge of the land No Name ruled, he smelled something on the wind.

8.

Oog and Groog were tending the fire and talking when the rain began to fall. It was a light rain at first; not enough to prompt the two friends to take any action to protect the fire.

By this time, Oog—who had spent more than two full revolutions of the stars with the People—had learned much about the different kinds of rain. There was mist (the air filled with fine particles of water that floated more than fell); drizzle (a light rain with sparsely placed small drops of water); mizzle (slightly heavier than a drizzle, but still with fine, small drops); rain (a medium amount of water falling from the sky in medium-sized drops); a scud (an unexpected and short-lived shower with heavy wind); a downpour (a heavy rain with larger drops); a squall (a downpour with strong, blowing winds); and a torrent (a heavy, drenching rain with the largest drops of all).

Oog had learned that the fire more or less tended to itself in anything less than a scud. In downpours, squalls, and torrents, the entire village was called to action, raising the roof and forming a human shield around the sides of the fire as the fire keepers fed it fuel.

Oog's primary responsibility for the fire had been to search for fuel: fallen trees, large branches, small sticks, and dried leaves. The leaves were usually a challenge given the wetness of the climate, but the rain falling now was the first in more than ten days, so the stores of dried fuel were full enough that Groog and Oog were taking a prolonged rest. As this rain was merely a mizzle, they stayed perched on their log.

"Why do you think it rains?" Oog asked.

"Ah," said Groog, "a very good question that I have often pondered."

"And?" Oog asked.

"I haven't thought of anything."

"Oh."

"What do you think?"

"Well, there is water in rivers, and water in lakes, and water comes out of our eyes. So, I wonder if there is a lake or river in the sky that we cannot see, or that perhaps a giant lives on the other side of the clouds and is crying."

"Interesting," Groog answered, "very interesting."

"So you agree?"

Groog thought for a moment. He held his hand out, catching some of the rain. He licked it with his tongue. "The water that comes from our eyes is salty. This is not."

"Then a river or lake in the sky?"

"But why can we not see it?"

"I haven't worked that out yet."

The mizzle grew to a steadier, heavier rain and the wind picked up.

Without exchanging a word, Oog and Groog rose as one and began to work the ropes that would raise the roof. It was just as Oog was pulling down on his end of the rope that he was hit in the back of the head with a rock. As he fell to the ground, he heard the bone-rattling scream of what sounded like a wild monkey.

9.

No Name had been watching the camp for most of a day. Two of his most trusted non-thinkers were with him. It wasn't that these non-thinkers were any smarter than the others, it was that they had been with No Name so long they had forgotten any other sort of existence.

The smell on the wind that had drawn No Name to this place was smoke. He had followed his nose to the edge of a clearing when he caught a glimpse of someone walking by scratching himself. It was an older man who seemed devoid of emotion or thought. No Name was just readying himself to assail the unsuspecting non-thinker, when he heard an unfamiliar sound and ducked behind a tree.

The old man, who was Grag, was not walking and scratching himself because he was a non-thinker; he was walking and scratching himself because he had someplace to be, and because his bottom itched. The latter was common among all people, thinkers and non-thinkers alike, in the Forest. There were many bugs, and many plants that left a residue. Scratching oneself, particularly on the bottom, was something of a national pastime.

The sound No Name heard was not Grag, but another person who had called to Grag. Unlike the grunts of the non-thinkers, and unlike his own strangled attempts at turning thoughts into sound, this was an organized, measured group of noises that, taken together, No Name understood to be speech.

His two aides took no notice of the sound. They simply scratched themselves and stole furtive glances at No Name, desperate to avoid giving his anger any reason to boil to the surface.

The person talking to Grag was Mother. No Name did not understand the words, but these were the sounds he heard:

"I am worried we have not had rain and am wondering if we should bring water from the stream."

Grag simply grunted in response.

Despite the non-thinking response from Grag, No Name recognized these people to be kindred spirits. They, too, had gone through the Change; they, too, could think.

No Name almost stepped out from behind the tree on instinct alone, screaming I am here! I am here! I am like you! But a life of dark actions and darker thoughts kept him rooted to the spot.

If these people can think, he reasoned, *then they will want what I have. They will want my non-thinkers for their own use. On the other hand, perhaps there would be something to be gained by treating with them. I shall watch,* he finally thought, *and wait.*

For hours No Name stayed hidden in the trees. Occasionally, one of the people would sniff the air and look in his direction, but none ever pursued the scent on the wind. In this manner No Name and his men remained unnoticed.

The first thing No Name realized was that these people, and there were many of them, were old. Very old. So old they walked stooped to the ground, the hair on their heads and bodies gray, gone, or both.

Then he saw Oog.

He is barely older than a boy, No Name thought. *What is he doing with these fossils? He must be their slave.*

No Name puzzled over this until his observation of Oog led him to discover something far more remarkable; the source of the smell that had drawn him here.

Fire.

The boy and a much older man stood over a circle of stones. At its center was a dancing orange and yellow light. The light, beautiful beyond anything No Name had ever witnessed, seemed to be eating trees and sticks.

If I have that, No Name thought, *I will be invincible.*

He nudged one of his aides in the shoulder, making him recoil. No Name grunted and pointed at the fire. Where he saw beauty and opportunity, the aide saw only terror. Before No Name could slap a hand over his lieutenant's mouth, the aide screamed in fright. The second aide looked up, saw the fire, and he too screamed.

Several of the people looked in the direction of the screams, but none came to investigate. *Their age has made them weak,* No Name thought to himself. *And that young one will be no challenge at all.*

No Name spent the next hour preparing for his attack. He gathered many rocks and with hand gestures showed his lieutenants what he intended. No Name's plan was to pummel the people with the rocks, and in the chaos, steal the fire. The lieutenants had learned to mimic rock throwing and seemed to grasp what their master wanted.

That was when rain began to fall. It fell lightly at first, but quickly grew heavy, pushed and pulled by the wind.

No Name was amazed as he watched the boy and old man pull a series of vines to raise a large square of animal skins. Fearing he would lose his chance to possess the fire, No Name let out an ear-piercing scream and hurled the first rock.

A practiced shot, he hit Oog in the back of the head.

In a flash, No Name and his two troops were darting across the clearing to the fire, throwing more rocks, screaming, and knocking down anyone who got in their way. As the three marauders reached the fire pit, No Name punched Groog in the solar plexus, knocking the wind from his lungs, and pushed him down. The rope slipped from Groog's hand and the tarp fell on the fire.

The falling tarp, a kind of fake sky that dropped inexplicably out of the real sky, scared No Name's aides beyond reason, and they ran. No Name, overwhelmed by the new and mysterious events, and having been abandoned by his lieutenants, had no choice but to run as well. He ran and ran, almost off the very edge of this story. Almost.

The People were in a state of disarray: several were injured, others ran in fear, Groog was on the ground, and Oog was unconscious. All the while, the heavy rain pelted the animal skins that now smothered the fire.

It was anarchy.

It was disaster.

It was the first glimpse of the hell that human beings had yet to invent.

It was a really bad night.

NOTES ON FIRE

Many thousands of years after Oog was bonked on the head, a group of pseudo-scientists will posit that fire is a living thing. They will claim it contains all of the basic attributes of life: it moves freely and independently; it needs oxygen; it feeds on organic matter; it can reproduce itself.

Most people will write the group off as a fringe element bent on forcing yet another lunatic theory down the throats of a weary and fatigued public. The group, with the remarkably unsubtle name of "Fire: Autonomous, Intelligent, Living," will publish a paper claiming to have devised a way of communicating with fire, this in spite of fire's lack of a brain, central nervous system, or vocal cords.

Snickering news anchors will later report—with no small amount of irony—that the entirety of the group perished in a raging inferno when their communal house burned down. These same anchors will also point out that perhaps the group shouldn't have chosen a name with the acronym FAIL.

When reached for comment, Fire was said to be saddened by the news, as it was really enjoying conversing with the pseudo-scientists just before it ate them.

10.

Oog was having what started out as a happy dream. He was bringing a bundle of sticks back to the fire, relishing the Forest around him. Small woodland animals scurried from bush to bush and jumped from tree branch to tree branch. Dappled sunlight, snaking its way through the overlapping leaves that formed the pate of the woods, found its way to the well-trodden path that led back to the camp. The aromatic smoke from the fire called to him the way a mother calls to her child.

He was even humming a tune, which was remarkable, as Oog had never before performed or even heard music. He was so taken with the sounds coming from his own throat—a kind of organized, guttural grunting—he didn't notice how dark and gray the sky had become. He didn't notice that the animals had vanished. Only when the scent of the fire turned acrid did Oog realize something was wrong.

He looked down and saw he was standing in water a foot deep, as if he had wandered into a lake or stream. Only he was not in a lake or stream. He was on the path back to the fire, back to Groog. A heavy rain, a torrent, began to fall.

The water was rising with great speed. First Oog's knees, then his thighs, and then his shoulders were under water. His hair was matted thick, and soon his ears were filling with the flood, rendering sounds muffled and distorted. He looked around for one of the People, but he saw none. He was alone, and he was about to drown, though he had no idea what drowning was. He simply knew he could not survive the rising tide of this new forest ocean.

As the water rose up to his mouth, Oog took his last gasp of air and went under. He tried to scream, but his throat and lungs were filled with water.

That's when Oog woke up.

He had a sharp pain in the back of his head. He blearily remembered how the rock had come from nowhere and brought him to the ground. When he looked up, the scene before him didn't make any sense.

Several of the People looked injured, or in some cases, dead. Mother was staggering over to him; a deep cut, crimson with blood, ran across her forehead. And that's when Oog noticed the fire. It was completely and totally under the tarp, which itself was covered in growing pools of water. Groog was on his knees, one hand over his midsection, grimacing as he tried to ease the tarp back and free the flames.

Oog screamed and leapt into action. He jumped to his feet, grabbed an end of the tarp, and pulled hard.

"NO!" Groog yelled, but it was too late.

As Oog pulled, the pools of water spilled from the top of the tarp onto the smoldering, though not yet extinguished fire. What little hope there was for rekindling the blaze from the hot coals was dashed as the rainwater poured from the tarp into the heart of the fire pit.

The People, those who were able, watched in horror as their fire, giver of warmth and light, cooker of food and heater of water, bringer of safety and security, was replaced by billowing towers of thick gray smoke.

"Gilligan!" someone shouted.

11.

The fire has gone out," Mother said. There were wails and cries all around.

"It's his fault!" Grag yelled, pointing at Oog.

Oog hung his head in shame as the murmur of the People, a murmur of agreement with Grag, grew louder.

"He was trained. He knew the dangers. He extinguished the fire!"

People wailed even as they bristled at the word extinguished, a profanity among their group. "His fault!" someone screamed. Another joined in until it became a chant. "His fault! His fault! His fault!"

For the first time since coming to live in this camp, Oog was frightened for his own safety.

"Enough," Mother said clearly and firmly. The chant died as quickly as it had begun, with a trailing "His fault," from Grag. "Enough," Mother said again, this time more softly. "This is not Oog's fault."

"What do you mean?" Grag shot back. "You saw him spill the water from the fire roof onto—"

"No," Mother answered. "I saw a band of non-thinkers attack our camp. Why this happened, I do not know. Perhaps our fire scared them. In any case, they are to blame for this. It is true that Oog did a poor job handling the roof, but it was in the confusion and chaos of the moment, and it was borne of a desire to help. Is that not so, Oog?"

Oog looked up but could not speak. He nodded. Groog placed his hand gently on Oog's shoulder.

There was some grumbling, notably from Grag, but the feeling of vilification, which had hung heavy on Oog a moment ago, dissipated like smoke on the wind.

"What do we do now?" cried one particularly gnarled woman. "How will we live without the fire?"

Mother thought for a moment before answering. "We must go and find fire and bring it back to our camp."

"But where, how?" one of the People asked.

"I do not know," Mother said.

There was silence.

A prolonged silence.

Birds tweeted.

Leaves on trees rustled in the wind, dropping fine droplets of water on the gathering.

Yes, even crickets chirped.

During this silence, Oog had a flash of memory. He would get these occasional flashes, like fireflies dancing across his mind, of the time before the Change, from the time before he could think.

More often than not, these memories took the form of feelings rather than sights, sounds, and smells. And most often the feeling was one of fear. But this memory was different.

Oog was young, very young. He huddled close to a female who nuzzled his head, her arm stretched around his small body. They had been sitting on the top of a hill, watching the dark of night slowly being erased by the light of dawn. The female, whom he was certain was his mother, raised an arm and pointed at the horizon, as if to draw Oog's attention there.

Oog was amazed at this memory for three reasons:

First, his mother was a thinker. She had deliberately tried to draw his attention to what Groog had called Nature. But if his mother was a thinker, what had happened to her? Why did she leave him? Or did he leave her?

The second amazing thing was that Oog remembered understanding. Had he, even at that very young age, had some nascent ability to think? For he recalled following his mother's outstretched arm and turning his full attention to the horizon, which is when the third amazing thing happened.

The very tip of the sun crested the horizon and the sky lit with flame, as if it was on fire.

It was on fire.

Of course, Oog thought to himself, *that is where fire comes from! The sun. When the sun rises every day, it drops fire. If I can go to the spot where the sun rises...*

He looked up. The People were staring at Mother, frightened at the realization that she, their matriarch, didn't know what to do. Oog heard the collective breathing of the group turn shallow, saw hands begin to fidget, caught a sob from somewhere behind him; the People were beginning to panic. He needed to do something.

"I know," said Oog with force and conviction. All eyes turned to him. "I know where to find fire."

• • • • • • • • • • •

The next morning, with the entire village gathered, Oog prepared to leave. The only possession he thought to bring was a sharpened stick, and this only because Mother insisted.

"You never know, dear, you never know," she offered cryptically, patting Oog on the shoulder.

With nothing to pack, Oog rose from his spot on the log by the now extinguished fire, turned to Groog, and looked him deep in the eye.

After Oog had volunteered to go in search of fire, there was discussion among the People, but no real debate. Oog could see that Groog had been troubled, but his friend held his tongue as the camp approved the plan.

Oog fell asleep that night dreaming of a grand adventure, battling and taming fire, and bringing it back to his family. Because that's what the People had become: family. But now, in the light of day, Oog found his resolve wavering. His mentor sensed this.

"I should go with you," Groog said.

Oog almost melted at the suggestion. Nothing would have made him happier in that moment than to have Groog accompany him. But Oog knew it could not be.

"You need to stay and help Mother watch over the People," Oog said, turning to Mother for support. She nodded.

"The People will be fine. I can—"

"No." Oog's interruption was firm. "I mean, yes, they will, but this..." He gestured at the now dormant fire pit, wondering why it seemed colder than the air around it. "This was my doing. I need to go on my own."

"But it will be dangerous."

"Danger is my middle name."

"Middle name?" Mother asked. "What is your last name?"

"What?" Oog said. "Oh...I have no idea."

Groog started to protest further, but Mother put a hand on his shoulder. "It has been decided," she said. Groog simply bowed his head. "May fortune smile on you, Oog Danger Last-Name-Unknown." And she, too, bowed her head.

Oog turned away from Mother and Groog and started off in the direction of the rising sun. The People formed a line along Oog's path, many of them patting his shoulder as he went by. He nodded and smiled at each as he went, trying to project as brave a face as he could.

Grag was last in line.

Oog stopped before Grag, searching for words to apologize for all he had done, but none came.

Grag, for his part, kept his eyes down, his foot nudging a loose stone. When he looked up, Oog could see wetness in the old man's eyes, and it made Oog's heart swell.

"Well," Grag said without a hint of emotion, "try not to die too horrible a death." Then he sneezed from all the ash still in the air, and turned to go, spitting on the ground as he did.

And with that, Oog was on his own.

12.

Oog's first few days of travel were both uneventful and frustrating. Each morning, he woke before the sun, hoping to catch the falling fire. And, each morning, he discovered the sun was still too far away.

He encountered no other people, thinking or not, which made him miss the people he'd left behind even more. Not for the first time, Oog wondered why he had not encountered any young thinkers. Mother had said that her tribe had all gained the power of thought at a young age. Given Oog's own experience, it stood to reason that all, or at least most, people went through the Change when they were still young. But if that were true, where were all these young thinkers?

"Maybe," he said aloud, "thinkers are dying off. Maybe I'm the last of my kind." The thought terrified him and he tried to push it away as he continued on his quest.

Oog ate berries, nuts, and leaves for sustenance, and drank from cool streams when he was thirsty. He slept under trees, his sharpened stick tucked at his side.

Just before the sun was at its peak on the fifth day of his march, Oog stopped in his tracks at the edge of a broad clearing. In the middle of the clearing stood the largest tree Oog had ever seen.

Though, of course, he could not be sure. Maybe he had seen trees just as large in the past, before he went through the Change. *That's a shame,* he thought. *How many things have I missed, simply from not being able to think?*

The tree was more than twenty long paces to walk all the way around its trunk. The branches—with wide, flat leaves of a deep and satisfying green—started low and continued so high that Oog could not see the top.

Groog would like to see this, he thought.

His memory of Groog made him homesick, which made him sad.

While Oog had been gone only five days, it felt like an eternity. He missed sitting and talking with Groog, he missed asking questions, he missed Mother and the other People. He even missed Grag.

No, he thought, I don't really miss Grag. *But I would still be happy to see him right now.*

Oog sat down, his back against the majestic tree, and started to weep.

As he wept, his eyelids grew heavy.

As his eyelids grew heavy and his tears dried, his breathing slowed.

As his breathing slowed, his mind cleared.

Oog fell asleep.

NOTES ON FEAR

A wise and great man named Franklin Delano Roosevelt once said, "We have nothing to fear but fear itself." He was trying to calm an anxious nation in the throes of economic collapse.

Roosevelt was raised with all the privileges society could heap upon a person. His gender, his race, his class, and his religion had subjugated all the other genders, races, classes, and religions to bend the world to their will. But a devastating disease had taught Roosevelt a thing or two about fear.

Meanwhile, another man, an army chaplain, one of millions of men fighting a great war on behalf of the nation led by Franklin Delano Roosevelt, is quoted as having said, "There are no atheists in foxholes."

A fox is a small omnivorous mammal.

A foxhole is a trench in the ground from which members of one army shoot guns at members of another army.

An atheist is a person who does not believe in the existence of a higher power.

While foxes do burrow in the ground, they rarely live in the same holes as soldiers with guns. And while atheists do sometimes carry guns, they rarely live in the same holes as foxes.

In any case, one soldier—a seventeen-year-old boy who had lied about his age to enlist, and who did not believe in God but who did believe in foxes, foxholes, and guns—is reported to have directly contradicted his Commander-in-Chief seconds before being shot by the enemy.

"Damn," he'd said, "all of these bullets and war and stuff are scaring me shitless."

The moral of this story is that perspective really matters, and that what happens in foxholes should probably stay in foxholes.

13.

Oog woke with a start when something sharp nudged his side.

He jumped up, disoriented, and found himself surrounded by fierce, unfamiliar animals.

Only, when he looked closer, he saw these were not animals at all. They were men wearing the skins of animals over their own skin and who had put color on their faces to make them look like animals. Each had bones in his hair, and each carried a big stick with a sharpened point. There were seven of them.

Oog was proud he knew there were seven men in the circle surrounding him. He knew this because Groog had taught him to count.

"What use is counting?" Oog had asked at the time.

"When you need it, you will know," Groog had answered.

Oog wondered if this was the kind of situation Groog was talking about.

Oog looked around for his stick but did not see it anywhere.

"Where is my stick?" he asked. On hearing Oog speak the animal men shifted from foot to foot, eyes darting to one another in what he recognized as fear.

Why do my words make the animal people uncomfortable? Oog wondered. *Maybe they mistook me for a non-thinker and I have surprised them*. He recalled something Groog had once told him: "Words, when used wisely, are more powerful than fists." Oog decided to put his friend's advice to the test. He squared his shoulders and faced the animal men, spreading his hands wide to show he was not a threat.

"Hello," Oog boomed, trying to smile as he did.

Again, the animal men squirmed and shot glances at one another, but none answered.

"Heeelll-looo," Oog said very slowly and very loudly.

Still, no response.

Oog was just about try again when he smelled something on the air. It had a flavor of rotted pinecones and bear piss, and Oog knew it to be the scent of danger. The short brown hair that covered much of his body stood on end.

There was a brief commotion as two more animal people—larger and more fierce than the seven already surrounding Oog—pushed their way through to the center of the circle.

One of the new animal men started screaming at Oog. "Docuit enim iniquitas arborem laedere!" Oog did not understand the words. They sounded like gibberish. He wondered if they sounded like the words he had shouted when he first began to think.

"I'm sorry," Oog said, "I do not understand you. Have you just learned how to think?"

The screaming animal man tilted his head in bewilderment. He looked at some of the other animal men in the circle, each of whom shrugged his shoulders.

"Magna arbor," the fierce animal man said, drawing out each word and pointing at the tree.

"Magna arbor?" Oog repeated, looking at the tree.

"Magna arbor," the fierce man confirmed, seeming satisfied that he had made himself understood. "Tangeret lignum vetitum!" he said, again pointing at the tree, and pointing down at the spot where Oog had fallen asleep.

While Oog didn't quite understand these new words, he was proud he was using his powers of thought to make sense of the situation and avoid an escalation of trouble. Repeating the first phrase of the fierce man—"magna arbor"—had worked once already, so he knew he should try again. He was only able to recall the first two of the three words the man had just used, but half a meal being better than none, Oog patted the tree, and with all the intensity the fierce man had used, said, "Tangeret lignum!"

All nine of the men with animal skins and pointed sticks gasped.

The fierce man shook his head and made a whistling noise with his mouth.

Oog was enthralled by the whistle. He was just beginning to purse his lips in imitation when he was bonked on the head, hard, from behind.

Everything went black.

14.

Oog was roused to consciousness by a searing pain on the back of his skull. "Wake up," the pain seemed to be saying, "and play with me." Oog groaned in response.

He was in some sort of cave made of rock, with walls on three sides. Through the open wall he could see it was raining. He remembered the day Groog had taught him how to catch rainwater, fashioning the broad leaves of a sycamore tree into a kind of funnel that would direct the water into a hollowed-out piece of wood. The memory filled Oog with melancholy. His heart felt like the rain: gray, wet, and altogether unpleasant. And his head felt like the cave: made of rock with a gaping hole in its side. Oog's wrists and ankles were raw and pink, and they hurt, almost as much as his head. He groaned again as he sat up.

"Easy, my friend."

Startled, Oog scooted back and hit his already throbbing skull on the low ceiling behind him.

"Ouch!"

"Please, do not be afraid. I am here to help you." The speaker, no older than Oog, was wearing skins and face paint, like the men who had encircled Oog by the large tree.

Oog was very confused.

"You...you...speak my words?"

"Yes," the strange animal boy answered. "I come from your part of the wood. I came here in search of answers and learned the language of the People of the Tree. Tell me, friend, what brings you here?"

While this boy was being very nice and pleasant, Oog neither understood what he was saying, nor did he trust him. He, Oog, had been hit on the head and brought against his will—or, at least, without his knowledge—to this cave. He needed to be cautious.

"You came in search of answers?" Oog asked, dodging the boy's question.

"Yes. I wished to understand nature and the true meaning of things. I wanted to know what happens when we die."

His curiosity piqued, Oog leaned forward. Despite the many illuminating conversations he and Groog had shared, he never felt comfortable with their conclusions. Nature is nature is nature seemed a wholly and completely unsatisfying explanation for the mysteries of the world. There simply had to be more. "Tell me," Oog said, his eyes closed in anticipation. "Have you found the answers you sought?"

"I have."

Oog opened his eyes wide to see the grin on his new friend's face.

"And can you...?" Oog swallowed. "Can you teach me?"

The young man clapped his hands together once in a display of joy. "That is precisely why I am here. I am to act as your interpreter and guide, and to help you learn the ways of the People of the Tree."

Oog realized his new friend had already used this phrase—the People of the Tree—to describe the men in animal skins, but he had no idea what it meant. He wondered if they lived in trees. But if they did, why was he, Oog, in a cave? Then he wondered if they ate trees.

Finally, he wondered if the people were not actually people, but some kind of walking, talking, head-bonking trees. All this wondering led him to the place it usually did¾a question: "What," he asked, "are people of the tree?"

"All of your questions will be answered tonight. In the meantime, I am here to tend to your wounds, and to provide you food and water." The stranger motioned to apples and nuts and berries, as well as a polished stone bowl of water. "But tell me, why are you here?"

Something in the way the question was asked had a pointed edge, like the end of a sharpened stick, and it reminded Oog to proceed slowly. "I am on a kind of quest."

"A spiritual quest?"

"Yeees," Oog answered, drawing out the word. "A spiritual quest."

"Then you've come to the right place."

This made Oog wonder if these People of the Tree had fire. They must. They knew the answers to so many things.

"Here," the stranger began, pushing the bowl toward Oog, and paused." I'm sorry, I realize I do not know your name."

"I am called Oog."

"And I am called Krog. Please, Oog, eat and grow strong."

And Oog did.

15.

At the exact moment Oog was being bonked on the head, Groog was arguing with Mother.

"It has been five days," he said, a crease in his brow. "He needs my help."

"Groog, please, it has been only five days. Oog may well be gone for an entire waxing and waning of the moon, or longer. We need to give him time and space to find his destiny. I am certain he is fine."

"He is not fine. I can feel it."

"You can feel it?"

Groog paused at Mother's question. His words were exactly the kind of nonsense at which he would have scoffed before all this madness befell the camp. It made him feel as if he was losing his mind. Groog had seen thinkers lose their minds before. They made strange guttural noises, tore at their own hair and skin, and sobbed uncontrollably. It was as if they had never been thinkers at all. Or as if they had thought too much. Either way, the prospect terrified him.

"Yes," he answered. "I feel it. Perhaps I've picked up a scent on the wind."

Mother sniffed the air and then looked at Groog through squinted eyes. "I only smell the sadness of the People."

"Well, then, perhaps it is something more...mysterious."

Mother looked askance at Groog. She had never known him to say such things. He had never known himself to say such things.

"I know, I know," he argued, hanging his head. "It doesn't make sense. I cannot explain it. I only know that I must find Oog, and I must help him."

"You are my oldest friend," Mother said, laying a gentle hand on Groog's wrist. "And you are the only other voice of reason here." She gestured to the broken camp of the People.

It was true. With the fire gone, with half the camp's inhabitants still injured from No Name's attack, an odd blend of panic and malaise had blanketed their corner of the Forest. When the People weren't openly sobbing or wailing, they were sitting in a catatonic state, staring at the now dry and ash-colored fire pit.

"We need you here," Mother said.

"The best way I can help them," Groog answered, waving a hand to take in everyone else, "is to help Oog and bring fire back."

Mother shook her head. "If you go, you will not return." Her voice cracked on the last word.

"I will return. I swear it."

"Do not, my oldest friend, make a promise you cannot keep. This I have foreseen. Leave now, and you and I will never see one another again."

Groog didn't know what to do. Mother's plea was strong, and he had known her for many more revolutions of the stars than he had known Oog. In the end, it didn't matter. Groog had to follow his heart.

Mother turned her back on Groog, a sign of her anger and her disappointment, and walked away. He let loose a heavy sigh, took one last look around, and walked out of the camp.

16.

Two glowing eyes peered down from a perch in a tree and watched Mother's camp. They watched and they waited.

If No Name had learned one thing as a thinker, it was that patience was indeed a virtue.

The attack on the camp had left No Name shaken. Until that moment, he had exerted almost total control over his actions and his surroundings. He had used his powers of thought to build his army, to instill fear in those around him, and to ensure he, No Name, never wanted for food or comfort.

Then he saw the fire and everything changed. He became a being possessed. No Name simply had to have that fire. And it was right there, those beautiful dancing flames, guarded by a group of weaklings; it was his for the taking.

But somehow, everything had gone wrong. The intensity of the rain, the terrifying false sky that came crashing down on the fire, the flight of his lieutenants; it was all too much, and No Name lost control.

Never again, he vowed, would he be so ill-prepared. Perhaps dealing with thinkers was more complex than dealing with non-thinkers. The idea made sense to him.

He returned to his army that evening, the sting of defeat

bringing out the worst in No Name. It was a long and miserable night for his soldiers.

The next morning, No Name set off alone to survey the encampment, hoping to once again spy the flames he coveted. He found a tree with low branches and climbed up high. It was a simple path to the top, until he looked down. No Name had never been up high before, and he didn't like it. But the reward, he kept telling himself, would be worth it.

He imagined all the things he would do with fire. He could use it to grow the size of his army. He could burn trees that got in his way. Fire could help him see better at night. He wondered if the fire was a thinker, too, and he harbored a small fantasy that he and the fire might become friends.

But now, from his perch near the top of the tree, he could see there was no fire. Only a cold pit of ash surrounded by small stones. His attention turned to the people of the camp; it appeared as if a kind of ceremony was taking place. The people were gathered in a line watching the youngest of their crew—the only one who could be described as young at all and one of the two who had tended the fire—walk out of the camp.

Using his power of thought, No Name wondered where the boy was going that warranted such an involved goodbye. Was this how thinkers always said goodbye? Was it how they said hello? If so, he wanted no part of it.

By the time the sun was high in the sky and the boy hadn't returned, No Name reached the conclusion that the boy had been driven away for causing the fire to go out. But what if I'm wrong? he thought. *What if he's being driven away to go in search of new fire?*

Torn between wanting to follow the boy and keeping watch on

the camp, No Name decided the elders of this village, who had probably been thinking for a very long time, would not put all of their trust in someone so young. Besides, if the boy was sent to fetch fire, he would bring it back and No Name would still achieve his goal. He chose to stay and watch.

By the fifth day, with no sign of either the boy or fire, No Name feared he had made the wrong choice. *I am young,* he thought, *I should have put my trust in this other young thinker. Let this be a lesson to never trust old people.*

He was just preparing to leave when he spied the other fire tender, a much older man, in a heated conversation with the woman whom No Name had observed to be the camp's leader. After the exchange ended—and No Name surmised it had ended badly—the old fire tender got up and walked out of the camp.

No Name would not make the same mistake twice. This time, he followed.

17.

Groog followed the trail left by Oog, finding broken twigs, snapped branches, and footprints made by his friend. Then, near the end of the second day, the trail went cold.

The clues had led Groog to a break in the trees, but no farther. Unsure of what to do, Groog continued in a straight line across the open space and re-entered the woods. As the day grew dim and lost its warmth, Groog saw no more signs that Oog had come this way. He was just starting to contemplate turning back when he caught a scent on the air.

Another person was near. The odor was familiar, and for a moment, his heart swelled. Oog, he thought. But as his nose took in more of the scent, he knew this was someone different. And if he wasn't mistaken, it was two someones.

He did a slow pirouette in a full circle, which was when he saw something most unusual.

It was a cave made of wood and thatch.

Groog walked around each side, marveling at the ingenuity of the construction. Fallen trees had been hewn into long, thick logs of equal length and stacked one on top of the other in an interlocking pattern, dried mud holding them fast at the seams.

"Fascinating," he muttered.

"Thank you."

The voice made Groog jump.

"I'm sorry," the stranger said, "I did not mean to startle you."

Groog smiled and bowed. "Groog," he said.

"Fred," the stranger said, bowing low himself.

Groog raised an eyebrow. "Is this your...cave, Fred?"

"It is called a house," Fred answered, "and yes, it is mine."

"Fascinating," Groog said again. "It protects you from rain and wind?" Groog circled the structure. Fred followed, the smile on his face betraying the pride he felt at Groog's admiration of his work.

"And from predators. And it keeps the cold at bay."

"Simply wonderful," Groog said, looking up and smiling at Fred.

"So, Mr. Groog, what brings you to this part of the wood?"

The question jolted Groog back to the moment. "Yes, of course. I am searching for my...wait. Is there someone else here?' Groog sniffed the air, certain there was a second person nearby.

"You know," Fred said, also sniffing the air, "I was going to ask you the same thing. Is there someone traveling with you?"

"No," Groog said.

The two men looked at one another, puzzled.

No Name, who was high in a nearby tree, could make no sense of the noises the two men made at one another, but he could see from their actions they were aware of his presence. He remained very, very still.

Fred looked in several directions and shrugged his shoulders. "Perhaps," he said, "it's a passing non-thinker."

"Perhaps," Groog answered. After the attack on his camp, which he believed had been perpetrated by non-thinkers, he was on edge.

"So, tell me, Mr. Groog," Fred asked again, "what brings you here?"

"Yes, sorry. I'm searching for my..." Groog hesitated, not quite sure how to describe Oog. In the end, he decided to follow his heart. "I am searching for my son."

Hearing this, Fred looked alarmed. "Oh dear, I see. How did you lose him?"

Groog told Fred the story of Oog. How Oog had come to him, how they had grown to be father and son, and how Groog loved Oog. He spared no detail in describing the attack on their camp, the fire going out, and Oog leaving on a quest in search of the rising sun.

Fred listened in rapt attention, the story more interesting and glorious than anything he had heard before. "I know this part of the Forest well," he said. "Maybe I can help you find his trail."

Relief flooded Groog's entire being. "You would do that?"

"Of course! What kind of world would this be if thinking beings didn't help one another?"

Groog, not sure what to do, stepped forward and grabbed Fred in an embrace. For both Groog, who was sad at the loss of Oog, and Fred, who had been alone for many years, the hug was filled with joy and catharsis.

"But it's already late in the day. Let's stay the night and set off in the morning."

Groog, who was old and who was tired from two days of walking, welcomed the invitation. He sat heavily on the ground. "Thank you," he said with both weariness and gratitude. "I would like that very much."

That night, Groog and Fred ate nuts and berries and drank a

liquid made of fermented apples that Groog found delicious, and which made him feel light in the head.

"Tell me of your village," Fred asked. And Groog did. He told the story of how he and Mother had tamed fire, and how the People had lived many years in happiness and peace.

The two new friends spoke of everything and spoke of nothing. Their conversation settled into an easy rhythm and pattern, as if they had known each other for years. Eventually, their talk took a turn to the philosophical.

"Nothing happens when we die," Groog said in answer to Fred's question about death. His assertion was made with confidence and certainty.

Fred was quiet for a long moment. "I see," he said. But the tone of his voice suggested that he did not see. Groog sensed this.

"Yes?" he asked.

"Well," Fred began, "how can you possibly know?"

"How can I possibly know what?"

"How can you possibly know that nothing happens when we die?"

"I have seen things in the Forest die. We all have. Nothing happens. They just stay there, slowly returning to nature."

Fred smiled. "Do you dream?"

Groog tilted his head, sensing a logical trap.

"I do."

"And are the dreams real?"

"No. They are dreams."

"How can you be sure? How do you know this is not a dream?"

Groog thought on this for a long moment. "So, what do you think happens when we die?"

"I do not know," Fred answered, scratching his bottom. "No one does. That's the point."

"But how do you explain what your eyes have no doubt seen?"

"It is true, I have seen bodies rotting on the floor of the woods. It is a horrific and immeasurably sad thing to see."

"But..."

"But I feel as if there might be something different, something more. That perhaps, somehow, the part of us that makes us who we are survives death. Have you never had such a feeling?"

Groog had never felt that way about death, but what Fred was describing was very similar to the feeling he had about Oog being in danger. That he somehow knew—when he could not possibly know—that bad luck had befallen his adopted son.

"Perhaps," Groog answered cautiously, "I have."

Fred smiled and popped another berry into his mouth. "And perhaps none of it matters. The most we can do is live the best life we can. Come, my friend, let's get some rest. Tomorrow will, I suppose, be a busy day."

Groog smiled in return and stretched his muscles as he stood. He entered the house and lay down, his mind still contemplating the words of his new friend, and fell into a deep and untroubled sleep in no time at all.

No Name, who could no longer see the men, stayed awake a little while longer. The stress he'd felt at having to remain hidden throughout the day seeped into the night as his shoulders sagged and sleep overtook him. The moment his head nodded, he fell out of the tree with a thud. Startled but uninjured, No Name sprang to his feet and ran deeper into the woods, terror in his heart.

Groog and his new friend Fred slept through it all.

NOTES ON RELIGION

New human thinkers in the Forest were notable for the number of questions they asked. Some of these questions ("What happens when I hit this animal on the head with this rock?") had answers ("The animal either dies or is so mad that it bites you and you die."). But other questions ("What is the meaning of life?") had answers that were not satisfying at all ("Acorns."). This almost invariably led most thinkers to invent some form of God.

What is the meaning of life?

"Only God knows."

Why does it rain?

"God is crying."

Why do my farts smell good while my droppings smell bad?

"I don't know, but I suspect this God person has something to do with it."

That God played a central role in the life of the Forest was all the more amazing because no one had bothered to tell Them about it. God had been on a fishing trip in the eleventh dimension, unaware that life had taken root in the Forest. When finally reached for comment on the varied systems of belief the beings of the Forest had created in Their honor, God responded with a quizzical, "Who's doing what now?"

DAY 7

18.

That same night, after Oog had eaten and rested, and after the rain had cleared, leaving a clean, wet smell on the wind, Krog told Oog they were to leave the cave and go to an important ceremony.

The cave was in the side of a cliff wall, perhaps two body lengths between the opening and the hard ground below. Aside from wondering how they had gotten him into the cave in the first place, being up high terrified Oog; he had steered clear of the cave's edge the entire day. The only other time he had been off the ground (that he could remember), he had climbed a tree to pick cherries. But that was a low tree with low branches, and even then, he had fallen out. The memory gave Oog an unsettled feeling.

"I think..." he began, in response to Krog's request that they leave the cave.

"...therefore I am?" Krog finished.

"What?"

"Nothing."

"No," Oog began again, "I think I am afraid of heights."

"Come here," Krog said, sliding forward on his belly, "look." Together, they inched to the edge of the cave's opening and peered down. There stood two long poles with a series of short poles binding them together.

"Is this some sort of tree?"

"It is a ladder."

"A ladder?"

"Yes, it is made from the wood of an already fallen tree. We use it to climb."

Understanding blossomed across Oog's face. *What an ingenious invention,* he thought. *Groog has got to see this.* "Wonderful," he whispered aloud, and started to move headfirst down the ladder. Krog caught his ankle and pulled him back.

"No, no," he said with a smile. "Feet first."

After several tries, and with Krog's patient and careful instruction, Oog made it to the ground.

"Now," Krog said, "before we go to the welcoming ceremony, you are going to need some clothes."

"I am sorry, I do not understand. What do I need to close?"

"No, no. Not close. Clothes." Oog blinked several times. "Skins, to cover your body, as I am wearing."

"Oh!" It was true; Krog wore the hide of a deer over his own skin. Oog could still smell the lingering scent of death and decay and fear on the skin, and he did not like it. "No, thank you," he said. "I am happy as I am."

"But all people here must wear clothes."

"What must they close?"

"Skins. I'm sorry, all people who stay here must wear skins."

"Why?"

"To not give offense to the Great Tree."

Oog knew what each of the words in Krog's sentence meant, but he did not understand the meaning of the words together.

"Follow me," Krog said.

Oog did.

After a short walk, they came to a small cave at ground level. Another animal man stood before the opening, holding a pointed stick in one hand and a rounded piece of wood in the other. The animal man exchanged a greeting with Krog and stepped out of the way.

Inside the cave were many wondrous things: animal skins, stone bowls filled with colored pigments, a large array of pointed sticks, and long, twining vines. These last items reminded Oog of the ropes they had used in his village to raise the roof. The sight of the vines made him unconsciously touch the raw, red marks on his wrists.

"What is this place?"

"This is our Thing Room," Krog answered.

"Your Thing Room?

"Yes, it is where we keep our things. Now, what kind of animal would you like to be?"

"I am sorry?"

"What kind of skin would you like to wear?"

"But I do not want—"

"Please, my new friend, humor me."

Krog had been very kind to Oog, and Oog did not wish to seem ungrateful.

"Then I shall let you choose," Oog said magnanimously.

"Hmm..." said Krog as he looked through the small pile of skins, selecting one after a long moment. "Yes, this one will do." It was hard and leathery and hairless, and smelled of pain and loss.

Oog did not like it. The skin frightened him, though he did not know why.

But Oog did not want to give offense. He put his head through the hole in the opening of the heavy skin and let it drape over his body. He could see, now that he was wearing it, how the skin was actually several skins somehow fused together. He looked at the place where the seams joined and felt along the edge. Small, stringy filaments had been used to make two pieces into one.

Everything that had happened so far and was happening now was too much for Oog's brain to process, and he began to swoon.

Krog saw this and brought Oog back out into the night air. "Deep breaths, my friend. You will be fine."

Oog took deep breaths and regained his footing, though he did not feel fine.

Still, he followed when Krog set off down a path and into the woods below the cliff.

It was a long, dark walk through a dense wood. Oog tripped and stumbled over brambles and rocks and fallen branches, the occasional moonbeams not doing enough to penetrate the tops of the trees and light their way.

"Is it much farther?" Oog asked more than once.

"We will be there soon," Krog responded each time.

Be where soon? Oog wondered. Everything about this place felt wrong. But if Groog had taught Oog nothing else, it was to question his feelings and trust his intellect.

Then again, these people had bonked Oog on the head. But so had Groog when they first met.

Then again, again, these people had done something to his wrists and ankles that was, in some way, connected to those human-made vines. But maybe Oog had frightened them. Though, if he was being honest, he could not see how.

Not for the first time, Oog questioned the usefulness of all this thinking.

At long last, Krog and Oog emerged from the woods into a clearing, at the center of which stood the most majestic tree Oog had ever seen. He recognized it immediately as the exact spot where he had first met the animal people. Those who he now knew were properly called the People of the Tree.

And, in fact, the people were now standing around this tree. They circled the giant trunk an arm's length apart, each with their legs shoulder-width apart, and each holding a pointed stick. And all of them together were humming and moaning softly, making the air alive with a kind of energy that both captivated and frightened Oog.

Now Oog understood. This was the Tree and these were its People. The People of the Tree. He was just trying to figure out what that actually meant when he and Krog arrived at the circle.

"Fratres," Krog said, "venite velit adiungere congregationesque."

Oog did not understand the words, but it was clear the others did. The circle widened and space was made for the two newcomers.

Oog followed Krog's lead and stepped forward. He looked at his new friend and saw his eyes were closed and that he had begun to moan like the other people. It was a freeform moan with no tune and no coherent organization. Not sure what else to do, Oog closed his eyes and began to moan along.

At first, Oog felt foolish moaning with his eyes closed in the middle of the Forest.

After a while, he still felt foolish moaning with his eyes closed in the middle of the Forest. He was concentrating so hard on the moaning, doing his best to fit in, he did not notice he was the only one still moaning until Krog gently jabbed him in the ribs.

When Oog opened his eyes, he saw that the collective gaze of the

People of the Tree was on him. There were too many to count, but Oog suspected there were at least one hundred. For someone who had only recently learned to count, one hundred was a very big number, indeed.

A larger and fiercer Person of the Tree—the same large and fierce animal person Oog had the misfortune of meeting the day before—started to speak. The words were like all the words these people spoke; lyrical and pleasing to the ear, but nonsensical.

"Grata, Fratres," the fierce animal man said.

"Welcome, brothers," Krog whispered, his words a beat behind those of the leader. Oog realized Krog was translating and was fascinated. "Tonight is a special night," Krog continued. "It is the annual Festival of the Moon. It is the night we recall the origin of the Tree and how we came to be in its service. It is a doubly special occasion, as tonight we also welcome a new brother."

All eyes turned to Oog.

Oog smiled.

No one smiled back.

The leader said more words of gibberish. But rather than translate, Krog repeated the words along with all the other people. "Omnis arbor adoremus."

"What?" Oog whispered.

"It means all worship the tree," Krog whispered back. "Don't worry, you'll get the hang of this soon."

The leader began to speak again, and again, Krog began to translate.

"Long ago, in the time before our fathers..."

'The time before our fathers?' Oog thought. *How long have these people been thinking? They must be very smart.*

"...there were two great beings. Conifo the man-tree and Decidua the woman-tree. They were fifty feet tall and had power over all things. They tended to the animals and the plants, they made the weather and the stars, and they spun the sun and moon around the sky. The world was a good and happy place.

"And then, came Man."

Several of the People of the Tree, including Krog, made a hissing noise at this part of the story. Wanting to fit in, Oog made a hissing noise as well, though it came out sounding more like a bumblebee.

"Conifo and Decidua tried to reason with Man," Krog continued, whispering his translation.

"'Man,' they said, 'we have dominion over all. We tend to the animals and the plants, and we make the weather and the stars. We spin the sun and moon around the sky each day. You will worship us, and we will provide for you as a mother and father would.'

"But Man, in his arrogance," Krog whispered, his own emotion caught up in the story, "refused.

"'This land belongs to Man,' Man said. 'This land is our land. From that tree over there, to that tiny, little island.'"

"That's got a nice ring to it." Oog whispered.

"What?"

"Those words you just said, they have a nice—"

The animal person to the right of Oog gave him an admonishing hush.

Krog began to translate once more. "Conifo and Decidua were confused. Never before had they been spurned by a creature of the Earth. 'But when you die,' they said, 'who will care for your soul? Will you wander in the wilderness, or worse yet, rot in the ground?'

"'I will take my chances,' Man answered, and spat at the feet of the two great trees."

Again, the people hissed.

"Then, before Man understood what was happening, Decidua bowed her head low as Conifo grew to three times his height, towering over and terrifying all. The animals hid, the plants quivered, and the weather grew dark, hiding the sun and the moon.

"Conifo scooped Man up as if he was a twig and looked the frightened creature in his tiny eye. 'You dare defy us? You will stand as a monument to your kind so they will know to bow before us. Only then will you be safe. Only then will you be cared for.'

"Conifo threw Man high and far into the air. For many, many miles Man sailed over land and sea. As he traveled, his skin turned to bark, his arms to branches, his hair to leaves. He landed with an explosive thud, his feet sinking into the ground and forming roots.

"We stand before you now, Man the Blasphemer," Krog pointed to the majestic tree, "to remind ourselves of your folly, and to worship Conifo and Decidua and all the trees."

"Omnis arbor adoremus" the People of the Tree intoned over and over, holding their hands over their heads and spinning slowly in circles. Oog said the prayer and spun with them. The ritual made him feel silly, afraid, and comforted all at once, and he could not explain why.

19.

Later, back in his cave, Oog stared at the ceiling as his mind replayed the events of the evening.

After the fierce animal man finished the story of Conifo and Decidua, Oog was formally welcomed to the community. The angry stares of the people turned to smiles and pats on the back. A feeling of warmth and love spread through his body unlike any he had ever known. Oog mentioned this to Krog on their walk back to the cave.

"That is the spirit of our gods filling you up."

"Gods?"

"Yes, Conifo and Decidua are gods. Do you not know this word?"

Feeling foolish, Oog shook his head.

Krog patted Oog on the back. "Do not be embarrassed, my friend. The people where you and I come from have yet to understand gods and the true nature of the universe. It is part of our mission to bring the word of the gods to all parts of the wood, but we can discuss that another time."

"But what is a god?"

"A god is an all-powerful, all-seeing, all-knowing being that created the world, and that protects us and all the creatures."

"And is it true, when we die, we go to live with these gods?"

Krog wore a paternal smile, much like the smile on Groog's face when he and Oog were discussing nature, and said, “Yes, when we die, we go to be with Conifo and Decidua, and they will care for us.”

This seemed too good to be true to Oog. But given his need for answers to the mysteries of life, the Forest, and everything, he allowed the idea in.

Before the circle had broken and the people had returned to their caves, the fierce animal man had told Oog (with Krog translating) a list of rules by which all People of the Tree must abide. “Failure to live by these rules will result in punishment swift and severe.”

Oog nodded, trying his very best to think and understand.

“First, and most importantly, you must never cause harm to a tree. And you must especially never cause harm to the Great Tree,” Krog translated, as the fierce animal man motioned to the tree before them. “We may only pick and eat fruit that has already fallen to the ground, and we may only use wood already surrendered by the Forest. We may never climb trees or remove branches, and we must never, ever light wood on fire.”

Oog kept silent about the true nature of his quest and let the leader, whose name he learned was Cagu, continue.

“Second, you will do your best to learn our language.”

“But wise Cagu,” Oog said, trying to be respectful, “I do not plan to stay here. I must return to my village.” Thoughts of home—of Groog and Mother and even Grag—trying to survive without fire made Oog feel as if his insides were being tied into knots.

Krog translated, prompting Cagu to respond with words Oog could understand perfectly, even if they were delivered in the manner of someone unfamiliar with Oog’s language.

“Everyone,” he said, “stays.” The smile on his face, his stained teeth bared, reminded Oog of a wolf.

"Third," Cagu continued with Krog once again translating, "you will always respect, honor, and obey the word of our elders.

"Fourth, when you stand before the Great Tree, you will do so in the guise of an animal, for to stand here as Man is to give offense.

"And finally, you will pledge to worship as we worship for the remainder of your natural life."

"My natural life?" Oog asked through Krog. He waited for the translation and answer.

"Until you die."

After Cagu had left, Oog tried to explain to Krog that he could not stay, that he had to fulfill his quest and return to his village.

"Tomorrow, my friend, we will discuss this all tomorrow." Krog led Oog back to his cave. Not wanting to set off at night, Oog decided to wait and see what tidings the morning brought.

But Oog was unable to sleep. The ideas of the People of the Tree were interesting. They provided answers for many of the questions that had plagued Oog since he first became aware of the world around him. But answers weren't of any value if they didn't make sense.

Trees, Oog thought, did not seem magical.

Trees seemed like trees.

Animals seemed like animals.

And people seemed like people.

Even people dressed like animals still seemed like people.

But what if their stories were true? What if these trees—Conifo and Decidua—really were gods? Perhaps they could help the people of his village. Oog was, not for the first or last time, very confused.

And then, just before the sun was due to rise, Oog smelled smoke on the wind, and everything changed.

20.

The morning after arriving at Fred's house, Groog woke with stiffness in his joints and not enough breath in his lungs. The chill air seemed to have settled in his bones.

I am getting old, he thought.

He enjoyed a long, leisurely stretch, moving every muscle in his arms, legs, back, and neck. While this brought some of the warmth back, for the most part, the chill remained. It made Groog long for fire. He hadn't realized just how much he'd missed it until this moment.

He looked around the inside of the hut, finding it the same as the night before with one notable difference: Fred was not there. Groog stood up, found the door, another marvelous innovation, and stepped into the morning light. Fred was peeling nuts and stripping berries from a branch.

"Good morning, my new friend," he said to Groog.

Groog returned the pleasantry with a smile, rubbing his hands together for warmth. He joined his friend, and the two ate a pleasant breakfast.

"Tell me," Groog asked, "do you have a son?"

"I'm not sure," Fred answered.

Groog cocked an eyebrow.

"Like your son, like many of us, I was not born a thinker. The gift came to me later in life. If I had any children, I know nothing of them. It is, perhaps, the greatest heartache of intellect—loss without having ever gained."

Groog thought on this for a while and saw wisdom in the words.

"Consider yourself lucky," Fred continued, "that you had Oog for the time you did." Fred saw the alarm on his friend's face and quickly added, "Which is not to say we won't find him. We will."

Groog nodded. "I just don't know where to begin."

"Take me back to the point at which you lost his trail."

The two friends finished breakfast and Groog led Fred back to the clearing and across to its other side, where Oog's trail had gone cold.

The clearing was an irregular shape, with tentacles of grass invading the thick stands of trees surrounding it. At its widest point, Groog estimated it to be eighty strides across, perhaps thirty at its most narrow. The two men turned slowly around, looking in every direction. Groog could see no discernible difference in the landscape, no matter where he looked. He let out a heaving sigh.

"There," Fred said after a long moment of silence, pointing across to the left side of the clearing.

Groog looked intently in that direction, shielding his eyes from the glare of the sun. "You see something?"

"What? Oh, no. But it's just as good as any other direction." He set off. "You coming?"

Not having a better plan, Groog followed.

21.

No Name waited for the men to cross the clearing and enter the woods before setting off in pursuit. He knew he needed to let them get far enough ahead that his presence would remain concealed. For all its ills, thinking had its benefits.

Then, before he could take a single step, his entire world went dark.

Something had been placed over his head.

Instinct took over and No Name thrashed and screamed, the terrifying screech causing birds to take flight, squirrels to scamper up trees, and one unlucky deer to run headlong into the trunk of a giant oak, knocking itself unconscious. When the deer woke, several hours later, it had become separated from its herd, and went on a grand adventure to find its way home. But that is a story for another time.

Groog and Fred stopped on hearing the scream.

"What was that?" Groog asked.

"Don't know," answered Fred.

Both men shrugged and continued on their way.

An instant after his first scream, a large hand clamped down over No Name's mouth, forcing him to taste whatever it was that covered his head. It tasted like a fox. Other hands, strong hands, grabbed each of his arms by the biceps.

"Quiet," a calm but firm voice said. "You are We now."

22.

Dag was born a thinker, and it was thinking that was getting her into trouble now.

The village from which Dag hailed was populated by a large group of diverse people, not all of whom were born thinkers. While the numbers of born thinkers increased with each revolution of the sun, nearly a third of newborns in the village still entered the world without the power of thought.

Each child in the village, regardless of the circumstance of their birth, was loved and treated as an equal. Dag grew up playing with thinkers and non-thinkers alike.

As was true in any society, the children of Dag's village would test the boundaries of acceptable behavior. This often took the form of born thinkers taking advantage of their non-thinking kin; they would trick them, humiliate them (though it is very hard to humiliate a being who is not self-aware), and sometimes even hurt them. When adults in Dag's village saw this happening, they would intervene. When they didn't see this happening, Dag wouldn't hesitate to point it out.

Dag loved her friends, those self-aware and those not, and she considered it a personal affront when one of the children endowed with the capacity for thought did something to demean a non-thinker. Dag's finely honed sense of justice had earned her the nickname "Little Fighter."

Which explained why Dag was so viscerally upset at the annual Shunning Ceremony.

Once a year, on the evening of the fall equinox, any member of the village who had seen seventeen revolutions of the stars and had not yet learned to think was driven into exile. The people, the thinkers, of the village formed a wall and forced the confused and terrified non-thinkers to leave. (Even the non-thinkers under the age of seventeen participated in the wall, mistaking the activity for a kind of game.) Those driven away would return over and over again, only to find that their families, the very people who had loved them from the day of their birth, had turned hostile. The exiled non-thinkers were denied food, water, and most tragic of all, love. Eventually, the banished non-thinkers gave up and left.

Each time Dag witnessed this grotesque spectacle, her heart grew heavier, and the fire in her belly grew hotter.

This year's ceremony was more than Dag could bear. One of her favorite people, Girl (non-thinkers in Dag's village were not given names, they were simply Boy, Girl, or sometimes Person), was among those being driven away. Dag and Girl had grown up together, had played together almost every day, had picked nits from each other's hair, and had snuggled together in cold weather. Dag loved Girl, and Girl loved Dag. She imagined they were sisters, and like any good sister, Dag would do whatever she could to protect Girl. Dag had to find a way to stop the people from driving Girl out.

She appealed to her parents for help.

"I'm sorry, love," her father told her, "there's nothing to be done.

Girl must leave."

"Why?"

"This is how it has always been and how it must always be."

"But why?"

"Because, if a person hasn't learned to think by the time they reach seventeen years of age, they never will."

"So?"

"I'm sorry?"

"So what? We love them and live with them as non-thinkers when they're sixteen. What's the difference if they're seventeen, twenty-seven, or seventy-two?"

"I'm sorry, Dag," her father said again, "we must evolve, so they must leave."

"What does that even mean?" Dag threw her hands up in frustration and stormed off. With her parents unable or unwilling to help, Dag took her plea to the village elders.

"I'm sorry, Little Fighter," the leader of the camp told her, "there's nothing to be done."

"Why?"

"This is how it has always been and how it must always be."

"But why?"

The elder smiled at her and put a gentle hand on her cheek.

Dag, her face flush with anger, stormed off.

When it came time for the Shunning Ceremony, Dag ran into the woods and hid behind a tree. She stayed there, crying, until she was sure it was over. But still, she couldn't let it go.

For three days Dag talked to anyone in the village who would listen. And while she found a few sympathetic ears, most of her comrades saw no reason to change their ways. "This is how it has always been and how it must always be," one after the other told her.

On the fourth day, Dag, who had run out of options, decided to take matters into her own hands. *If they will not care for Girl and the others,* she thought to herself, *then I will.* She dropped what she was doing (whittling a stick with a sharpened stone), created a torch from the communal fire, and walked into the Forest without looking back.

Dag left in the same direction she believed Girl had walked—the non-thinkers were always driven out of the camp toward the setting sun—but having no real knowledge of how to track people, she lost Girl's trail after only a day. As the light seeped from the sky, Dag decided to stop for the night. She found stones and fuel and used her torch to light her own campfire, building it to a roaring blaze just before sleep took her.

In the morning, she made another torch, extinguished the remains of the fire, and continued on to the West. She foraged for food, found water when she could, and lit a fire each night from the torch. Seven days later, Dag had not encountered another living soul, and what was worse, she realized she no longer knew the way home.

Dag emerged from the Forest into a clearing, at the center of which was the most majestic tree she had ever seen. What a wonderful place to camp, she thought.

And that was how Dag came to be roasting a rabbit over a fire in the shadow of the Great Tree.

23.

Someone was burning wood.

They were not supposed to be burning wood.

No one was supposed to be burning wood.

There was no greater offense to give the Great Tree, or to the People of the Tree, than burning wood.

But the fire smelled good. It reminded Oog of Groog. It reminded Oog of home. It was the first time Oog had given serious thought to the concept of home.

Did he have a home?

What was a home?

Home, he thought, *is where the fire is. I must remember to share that with Groog.*

More to the point, if fire was nearby, Oog could tame it and bring it back to the camp, fulfilling the purpose of his quest.

He crawled quietly down the ladder outside his cave, donned the skin of an animal, and walked into the wood, toward the smell.

When he reached the edge of the clearing in which the Great Tree stood, Oog stopped.

Sitting under the Great Tree, roasting a skinned rabbit over a fire, was a female.

Oog did not need to be a thinker to notice females. He spent many sessions with Groog asking about females, all of which amounted to the same basic question: "Where can I get one?"

"You cannot get one," his older and wiser friend told him. "They are people just like you and me."

"No," Oog had said with force. "They are people, but they are not just like you and me."

Oog knew that he did not smell nice. He did not have the bumps on his chest. He did not make other people want to cry and laugh and sing all at the same time. (Well, he did seem to make Grag want to cry, but for wholly and completely different reasons.) "Ah, youth," was Groog's only answer.

The female he was staring at now, the one beneath the Great Tree, did all of that and more to Oog. He ducked behind a birch at the edge of the wood and watched, unwittingly violating a lesser rule of the People of the Tree: Thou shalt not hide behind trees.

He figured the female to be about his age. She looked confident and self-assured, but lonely, too. He also knew she was in danger. If the People of the Tree discovered her fire, she would be punished. He must help her. Then, together, the two of them could transport the fire back to the People.

Not wanting to scare the female, Oog set off across the clearing waving his arms and screaming, "Hello! Hello there!"

The female stopped what she was doing, stood up, and watched Oog, her head tilted in curiosity.

Oog stopped ten feet short of her fire, held his arms out in a show of friendship, as Groog had taught him, and, not knowing if she spoke his language, said, very slowly, "Ooooog." He patted his own chest and smiled. "Friend."

The female did not smile back. In fact, she frowned.

Bile rose from Oog's stomach in a panic, causing both the bile and the stomach to want to get as far from the unfolding scene as possible. He tried again. "Oooooog," he said emphatically, thumping his chest. "Frieeeeeend."

The female shrugged, touched her own chest gently, the motion sending a quiver down Oog's spine, and said, "Dag."

"Daaaag," Oog said slowly, and smiled, being sure to show all his teeth.

"Look," Dag said, "is there something wrong with you?"

Caught off guard, Oog cleared his throat. "What? Oh dear. I thought perhaps you didn't speak my language. Listen, you cannot have that fire here, you have to—"

But his words were cut off when Dag's eyes went wide. "Look out!" she screamed.

Oh no, Oog thought, *not again,* as he was bonked on the head from behind and fell to the ground unconscious.

NOTES ON IMPRISONMENT

The first attempt by one person to imprison another happened one hundred years before the time of Oog in another part of the Forest. Two new thinkers were having a disagreement over the creation of a word to describe a small, furry creature that ate nuts and scampered up and down the trunks of trees.

"We should call it a squirrel," the first new thinker had said.

"Squirrel?" replied the second new thinker with obvious disgust. "That has got to be the dumbest word ever spoken."

"This from the man who named 'tree sap.'"

"What's wrong with tree sap?"

"Sssssaaaaapppp. That's what. Anyway, I suppose you have a better suggestion?"

"Than squirrel?"

"Yes, than squirrel."

"I don't know, how about something with a little flair. Like maybe... Twizzlevarmint."

"Twizzlevarmint?"

"Yes, Twizzlevarmint."

"You're an idiot."

"You know, I've had just about enough of you."

"Oh yeah?"

"Yeah!"

The second new thinker then bonked the first new thinker on the head with a big stick. While the first new thinker was unconscious, the second new thinker bound his adversary to a tree with vines of ivy and walked away.

Since this confrontation happened before the invention of knots, and since the second new thinker hadn't stayed to stand guard, the first new thinker, after regaining consciousness, simply stood up and left the tree. Later that same night, he beat the second new thinker to death, effectively ending the first experiment in incarceration and cementing the word squirrel as part of the vocabulary for future generations.

After this initial failure, the nature and manner of imprisonment became more sophisticated, which turned out to be very bad news for Oog and Dag.

24.

Oog dreamed.

He had dreamed many times in his life. There was the nightmare that had led him back to consciousness the day the fire went out. There was the recurring dream in which he walked in circles and could not stop, no matter how hard he tried. But most often his dreams reverted to his more primitive history of chasing food, or of being chased by something that thought he, Oog, might be food. During these dreams, his legs and arms would move in small running motions.

But tonight's dream was different. He and the female, Dag, were on a windswept beach, holding hands, and watching waves roll in. The sky and ocean weren't just big, they were enormous. But with his hand warmed by Dag's, he felt grounded, safe. This was made all the more remarkable by the fact that Oog had never heard of, smelled, nor seen an ocean.

When he woke, Oog knew, though he could not explain how or why he knew, that the dream was not real. Still, he needed to tell someone right away. It was so beautiful and so fulfilling.

Only, when Oog tried to sit up, he could not. He was lying on the ground, his wrists and ankles bound to stone pillars. He turned his head and saw Dag next to him in the same predicament.

She was crying.

"Are you hurt?" he asked her gently.

Dag shook her head no.

Oog struggled for something to say, but did not know what. He had no experience talking to girls, nor did he have experience being bound to stone pillars. He most definitely did not have experience talking to girls while bound to stone pillars.

He looked around and saw a Person of the Tree standing a few feet away, dressed in animal skins and holding a pointed stick.

"Placere," Oog said, recalling one of the words he had heard Krog use. "Please."

The Person of the Tree, who was wearing the skin of a bear, turned to look at Oog, but otherwise ignored him.

"Placere," Oog tried again.

And again, no response.

"What words are you speaking? What is this place?" Dag asked.

Oog looked back to her. How to explain all of this? "These people," he said, "believe that the trees are gods, and they worship them, and that when you die you go to live with great trees in the sky."

Dag paused a moment, then burst out laughing through her tears. "Really. Live with trees in the sky? Really?" She sniffled. "You're just trying to cheer me up. C'mon, who are they?"

As Oog heard his own words through Dag's ears, he realized how silly they sounded. But now it was too late. He was trapped, and this beautiful female was trapped with him. It was all his fault.

Oog began to cry.

"Hey, don't do that. It'll be okay," Dag said.

But Oog could not stop crying. He cried so hard he did not see the bloodied, pointed stick come out through the chest of the guard. Nor did he see the man in the animal skin untying Dag. It was not until his own binds were loosened and he was once again standing that Oog realized he was being rescued.

"Krog!" Oog said with joy and hugged his friend.

Krog hugged Oog back.

"But wait," Oog said. "The People of the Tree will be very angry with you for killing this guard. And, now that I think about it, for freeing us."

"That is what I love about you, Oog. Your grasp of the obvious."

"Hi," Dag said, "I'm Dag."

"Hello, Dag, I am Krog. And we need to go."

"Please," Oog said, "tell us what is going on."

"Yes, but let's leave this place first. As you point out, these people will be none too happy. As soon as it's discovered I've helped you escape, they won't rest until they find us. Come on now, time to go."

Krog set off at a quick pace, Oog and Dag following close behind.

While he could not take his eyes off Dag—whose long, lean, and muscular legs ran just in front of him—the pain in Oog's head, where he had been most recently bonked, throbbed with each step.

The pounding in his skull made it hard to think, but he tried nonetheless. He had so many questions: Why did Krog betray the People of the Tree? Why would the People of the Tree not rest until they—Oog, Krog, and Dag—were found? Where did Dag come from and why did she smell so damn good? Why did his third leg stir every time he thought of Dag? Why had no one invented a better name than "third leg?"

I must think of a name myself, Oog thought as he ran. A clever name. But what? Oog gave the matter deep consideration but could come up with nothing better than "third leg." Not finding inspiration in the woods around him ("tree limb" felt particularly uninspired), he gave up, deciding in the end, and for no good reason he could articulate, to call his third leg Willy.

After being on the move for what felt like most of the afternoon, Krog slowed to a trot, his nose in the air.

Oog smelled it, too.

Water.

A few moments later, the three companions were squatting by a stream, dunking their heads, drinking, and laughing between breaths.

Krog looked down and noticed he was still wearing his animal skin. He pulled it over his head and tossed it in the river. "I always hated that thing."

"I do not understand," Oog began. "I thought you loved being a Person of the Tree."

"An intelligent being can only go on fooling himself for so long before it either catches up with him or he goes crazy."

"How long were you there?" asked Dag.

"Two revolutions of the constellations."

Oog and Dag look at each other and then at Krog in amazement.

"I know," he said before they could respond. "It caught up with me, and then I went crazy. I was so desperate for answers I would've believed anything. Seeing how they treated the two of you opened my eyes wide enough to know it was time to leave."

"Answers about what?" Dag cupped her hands to take long draughts of the cool water.

"Everything."

Oog saw Dag smiling at Krog and his hair stood on end, but not in a good way. "So," he interjected quickly, "what next?"

"Hmmm...I hadn't thought that far ahead."

"I need to get back," Dag said. "I wandered too far and lost my way. I need to get back to my part of the Forest. My family will be worried."

"Family?" asked Oog.

"My mother and father."

"Oh," he said, disappointment in his voice.

Dag and Krog were quiet, staring at Oog.

Oog noticed his friends' concern. "I don't know who my mother and father are."

"That man you spoke of..." Krog said.

"Groog?"

"Yes, Groog. He was not your father?"

"No." Oog looked thoughtful for a moment. "But I imagine he treated me the way a father would treat a son."

"You don't know your parents?" Dag asked.

"I did not start thinking until recently, so I have no idea where my parents might be."

"You could look for them," Dag offered hopefully.

"What would we even say to each other? 'Hi, I'm Oog, your son, and I think.' And they'd say 'Googo gorogooorg fafoego gagog?' And then bonk me on the head?"

"A mother knows her son. By instinct."

"Are you a mother?" Oog asked.

"Me? No, I've only been alive for sixteen years."

"Years?" Krog and Oog said together.

"Revolutions of the constellations."

"Oh!" Oog answered excitedly. "What a wonderful word. Years." He sounded it out. "Yee-ers."

"Years," Krog said the new word carefully.

Talk of family and home and words brought Oog's quest crashing back to his consciousness. "Fire," he said to Dag. "Can you make the fire again?"

"No. I brought a torch with me when I left. Why?"

"That is why I left my camp. Our fire went out and my people will die if I don't find a way of returning with a flame."

"Please," Krog said, looking pale, "no more talk of fire." Oog and Dag looked at their new friend in confusion. "I spent two years with the People of the Tree, and there is no greater offense than fire."

"But fire is a giver of life," Dag said.

"Please, just give me some time."

Dag shrugged. "Okay, but what do we do now?"

"We help you find your way home, I take some of your," Oog paused, looking sideways at Krog, "burning wood?" Krog winced even worse. "And return it to my village."

"And what of Krog?" Dag asked.

"He will be welcome to live with me." Oog wasn't sure that was entirely true, but he would have to make it so.

The three friends nodded in agreement and set off on an uncertain path toward their uncertain future...uncertainly.

25.

No Name was forced to march through the Forest. The fox thing still covered his head, and his hands were bound behind his back, causing him to stumble more than walk. He tried to use his power of thought to gauge if they were turning left or right, going up or down hills, so that he might find his way back, but it was no use. He was thoroughly disoriented.

He was accompanied by two men; he could tell their number and gender by their scent. He could also tell by the size of their hands that they were larger than him. They jabbered at each other with their nonsensical sounds from time to time, but mostly stayed silent.

They traveled like this for what seemed to be a very long time.

No Name was certain he was being punished for his actions. For tricking and mistreating non-thinkers, for coveting fire, for spying on people. He was, for the first time in his life, filled with remorse. It was a new and alien emotion, and No Name didn't like it. Curse all this thinking, he thought. Just let me go back to the way things were.

His nose stirred him from his dismal reverie. He was suddenly aware of more people. Many more.

His captors grabbed his arms, halting his march. The fox thing was removed from his head, the light stinging his eyes. With his hands still tied, he could only bow his head and squint his sight back to normal. When he looked up again, he couldn't believe what he was seeing.

There were a dozen false caves, like the one the two men had disappeared into just before No Name had fallen out of the tree. Only, where that cave was made of wood, these were made from the skins of animals.

Moving into, out of, and all around the animal-skin-caves were more than a dozen people busy at various tasks. Each was young and muscular, and all wore animal skins to cover their bodies. There were as many people here as had been in the village of the old people, only where those people seemed docile, these oozed a kind of purpose laced with hostility. Most terrifying of all, each person had smeared some kind of red pigment on each cheek and forehead. At first he thought it was blood, but when he looked closer, he realized it was the juice of raspberries. *Do they want me to think it's blood?* No Name wondered. *Or are they just messy eaters?*

It was all too much. In a day filled with firsts, No Name, for the first time in his life, fainted.

26.

Cagu stood tapping his foot as he looked at the dead guard. In his ten years as leader of the People of the Tree, Cagu had never lost one of his men. Admittedly, this particular guard, his nephew, wasn't especially bright. In fact, he was the very first person to believe Cagu's fantastic tale about tree gods.

Cagu had invented the story of Conifo and Decidua to please and amuse his young nephew, then only a boy, and to help him fall asleep. Only the kid wasn't amused, he was enthralled. He walked around the following day, dropping to the ground and laying prostrate each time he came to a tree. Since they lived in an area populated with many trees, the boy spent most of the day on his stomach. Cagu approached his sister, the boy's mother, hoping she would talk some sense into her son.

"Listen, sis, about Cassius and this lying on the ground business—"

"He told me!" Cagu's sister's voice was filled with reverence. "I am so proud they chose to deliver their message to you."

"I'm sorry, what?"

"The tree gods, choosing my baby brother! Who would have thought it?"

"But the tree gods are—"

"All-knowing and all-powerful! Cassius told me." She leaned in and whispered in a conspiratorial tone. “Listen, can you tell me more? What else did they say?”

Cagu didn’t know what to make of this. He agreed that the very large tree near where they lived was special. It was older and bigger than any tree in the Forest, which imbued it with an air of wisdom and magic. And while Cagu knew these things—wisdom and magic—were projected on the tree from a lack of understanding, his nephew’s and sister’s reactions to his story made him realize the tree was also, perhaps, fertile ground for the creation of myth.

He tried his tale about Conifo and Decidua on three other people. Two of them believed it instantly. The story answered their most profound questions and helped ease the fears they had about the world. How could it not be true?

The third person to hear the tale shrugged and walked away. He would be exiled from their community within the year.

Cagu’s tale spread and, in less time than the waning and waxing of the moon, what had started as a few believers swelled to more than a hundred. Seizing the opportunity, Cagu added to his invention. He gave the myth depth and meaning, he created rituals, and he periodically retreated to a remote part of the Forest, atop a large mountain, where Conifo and Decidua “spoke” to him, handing down laws and rules by which the people must live their lives.

It was all so easy. So very, ridiculously easy.

The people hung on Cagu’s every word. They gave him extra food and clothes. And the sex. Holy cow, the sex. Things were so good he sometimes wondered if Conifo and Decidua were actually real and somehow looking out for him. Then he’d catch himself and laugh. *If I can keep a level head,* he thought, *and remember this is nonsense, I can run this scam for years.*

And he did.

For ten years the People of the Tree lived in harmony and obeyed his every command. No matter how silly, they did it.

Don't burn wood. Okay, we won't.

Wear animal skins. Sounds good. We will.

Twirl in a circle with your hands over your head. You didn't say Simon Says, but sure, we're all-in on this tree business.

It's good, Cagu thought, *to be the king.*

But now, something had gone wrong. Something had gone terribly wrong.

The outsider, Oog, had infested the minds of his people with heresy, and now Cagu's nephew was dead, and one of his most trusted disciples, Krog, was gone.

Two other guards—rugged men with animal skins, wooden shields, and sharpened sticks—were with him at the scene of the crime. Cassius's body lay where it had fallen, a spear through the chest. A muddle of footprints led away from the camp. Cagu took one more look at his fallen nephew and gave the order.

"Inveniemus eos et occidet illos. Veni, oportet nos parare." We will find them and kill them. Come, we must prepare. Cagu set off, the guards hot on his heels.

27.

Moments after Cagu left, two trees—not as large as the Great Tree, but each a sight to behold in its own right—pried themselves from the forest floor and stood on their roots.

"Come, my love," said the first tree in a deep, resonating voice, no mouth visible on its bark.

"Yes, Conifo, my heart," said the second tree, following a bit behind.

The two trudged off in the direction Cagu and his men had marched. They moved slowly, purposefully, patiently; as if they had all the time in the world.

Which they did.

NOTES ON THE FOREST

The Forest was a big place. Not as mind-numbingly big as the universe, or as brain-stretchingly big as a planet, or even as foot-achingly big as a continent, but to the inhabitants who lived there, the Forest was big indeed.

The only creature to ever successfully traverse the full length and breadth of the Forest was a Speeder Snail named Ryan.

The border on the eastern edge of the Forest—the indigenous home to the largest population of these fist-sized, fast-moving mollusks—was defined by a cliff with a sheer drop of precisely one hundred and fifty feet. This was known to the Speeder Snails as the Great Snail Swallower. At the bottom of the cliff was a river that frothed with whitewater.

By a strange coincidence of evolution, or perhaps as the result of a well-timed cosmic joke, the sound made by the water rushing over the shallow stones of the riverbed, when heard from a distance of precisely one hundred and sixty feet, was identical to the mating call of the Speeder Snail.

These clever little creatures, known as much for their libido as their hustle, would round a corner, hear the faux mating song, misjudge the distance to the edge, and plummet to their deaths. The only reason the entire species didn't die off was due to another strange coincidence of evolution. Over the millennia, the shell of the Speeder Snail had hardened to the point of being actual stone. This allowed a handful of them to survive the fall, though it rendered them sluggish and slow for the remainder of their days.

Ryan the Speeder Snail was oblivious to all of this. Like most of his brethren, he, too, heard what he mistook for his species' mating song coming from the river, and he, too, rushed recklessly to the edge of the Great Snail Swallower. Only, at that exact moment, a mammal resembling a very large squirrel fell out of a tree directly in Ryan's path. The large squirrel-like mammal was, inexplicably, holding a small sign that read "Death to the Queen."

Ryan was so startled by this he turned and ran, or rather, slithered, in the opposite direction and didn't stop moving until he had, unwittingly, reached the western-most edge of the Forest. It was there, having completed his historic journey, that he was eaten by a hedgehog, whose name was also, coincidentally, Ryan.

Speeder Snails play a very small but very important role much later in our story. So much later you will have forgotten they even exist by the time you get there.

28.

The next morning was beautiful. Sunlight shone through the trees making mottled patterns on the forest floor. The air was crisp and clean and filled with the sounds of birds and bees doing what birds and bees do.

Oog, Krog, and Dag walked three abreast, picking their way over logs and bramble.

"So, let me get this straight," Dag said to Krog as they walked, "you left your part of the Forest in search of...answers?"

"That's right," Krog said. "I suppose many of us are wanting to know what this," he made a big gesture, taking in the woods and all beyond it, "means."

"Means?"

"Yes. Answers to questions." Krog responded.

"I don't understand. What questions?"

"Like wanting to know what happens when we die," Krog said.

"Why?"

Krog looked at Dag, confused, and then looked to Oog for support. Oog shrugged his shoulders.

"Why do I want to know?"

"Yes, why?" Dag asked.

"Because I do not know."

Dag shook her head and was about to probe further when

someone stepped out from behind a tree, startling all three of them.

"Hi there!" It was a man, slightly built, and wearing an animal skin to cover his body.

Krog, who had thought to bring a pointed stick, pointed it at the newcomer.

"The People of the Tree," Krog observed with cool detachment.

"What people and what tree?" the man asked brightly, seemingly unfazed by the pointed stick.

Oog, Krog, and Dag exchanged a bewildered glance.

"Are you not one of the People of the Tree?" Oog asked.

"I'm sorry, I don't know what you're talking about."

"But you're wearing an animal skin."

"Yes," he said. "It gets cold at night."

Oog realized that since he had set off from his village the temperatures had been growing steadily cooler. He wondered if each person experienced the same temperature, or if your personal temperature was related to your distance from home.

Krog relaxed his posture, lowering the stick, but keeping it ready just in case.

"Then what are you doing here?" Dag asked.

"I like you!" the man said to Dag, smearing a dab of green paint on her shoulder.

"Hey!" Dag exclaimed.

Oog noticed the man had little dabs of green paint all over his body.

"Do you like me?" the man asked.

"What?" Dag was unsure of how to answer.

The man frowned. "It is customary in this part of the wood that when someone likes you, you like them back."

"Why?"

"Isn't being liked what life is all about?"

"Are your people near here?" Krog asked.

"Sure," he answered, "just a little ways over there." He motioned to a short rise in the land beyond a thicket of trees.

Krog looked at Oog and Dag. "We left in a hurry, and we're going to need food and water."

"Awesome," the man said. "But you do like me, right?" He held out his hand revealing a small pool of green dye.

Krog shrugged, stuck his finger in the dye, and dabbed the man on one of the spots on his skin not already covered in green. Oog and Dag followed suit. "Sure, we like you," Krog said.

The man chuckled with a strange kind of relief. "Awesome!" he said again. "Follow me. Everyone will be so happy to meet you."

The very cheerful man led Oog, Krog, and Dag a short distance to a fence made of cut logs. It stood just above the height of Oog's head.

"Hi!" the man called to a woman sitting atop the fence. It was a larger structure than Oog had ever seen. He paused for a moment to take it in. Logs lay horizontally, one on top of the other, but somehow didn't fall. How many people, Oog wondered, did it take to make this? I must remember to bring Groog here.

The woman sitting on the fence wore an animal skin, and the visible parts of her arms and legs were also covered with many green dots. "It's me, Jag!" the man continued. "The most popular guy in town!" He turned to Oog, Krog, and Dag and winked. Oog and Krog laughed nervously; Dag rolled her eyes.

The woman jumped down and pushed a section of the fence inward.

"Fascinating," Oog and Krog said together, looking at the small logs that had swung away from the rest of the wall.

Jag motioned them forward. "C'mon, let's introduce you around. I'm sure everyone will like you."

By the next morning, Oog had enjoyed a good meal, had relished a good night's sleep, and had quickly immersed himself in the life of this strange village. It was an impressive place, with caves made of wood and thatch. These people, he believed, must be very smart. And best of all, unlike the People of the Tree, the People Who Liked Other People, which is how he thought of them, made Oog feel welcome. His arms and neck were now covered in green dots, and a small bucket filled with green pigment was slung from a strap around his shoulder.

Dag, who had kept mostly to herself, sat on a log staring at Oog as he approached. "Really?" The tone of her voice vibrated with disapproval.

Oog looked at the green paint splattered on his body and then back to Dag. "But...but...people like me."

Dag looked down at her own body and animal skin. Only one green mark, placed there by Jag the day before, was visible. "And you don't think they like me?"

"Hey!" a passing man said, "I really like you!"

"I like you, too!" Oog said, already responding on instinct.

"Great!" The man dabbed Oog with green paint. Oog looked at Dag in momentary dismay before dabbing the man back.

The man turned to Dag. "I like you, too." He moved to dab her with paint, but she leaned back, making it clear she wanted no part of the pigment on the man's finger.

"Thanks," Dag said dryly.

"You know," the man said, "you could learn a lot from your friend, here." He stormed off.

Dag looked at Oog with a raised eyebrow. "Doesn't this seem, I don't know, a little silly?"

"I'm just trying to fit in."

"Hey!" Krog said, walking up, covered nearly head to toe in green dots. "People here really like me!"

"Oh, for crying out loud." Dag stood up and stomped away.

"Where are you going?" Krog asked.

"To find the person in charge."

"Why?"

"Maybe they can help me find my way home." She turned and kept on walking.

"Wait," Oog called after her, but Dag didn't break her stride.

"Don't worry," Krog offered, "she'll come around. Hey!" He had spotted a green-covered person passing in the distance. "I really like you!" He hurried off in pursuit.

29.

Traveling through the Forest grew more difficult for Groog and Fred with each passing hour. The trees grew closer, and the bramble that had been in sparse patches on the forest floor, grew thicker.

"I'm not sure we're going to find anything this way," Groog said as they stopped to rest. He sniffed the air. "Though I do think there's water near."

Fred raised his nose, too. "I believe you may be right. Let's find its source and then decide what to do."

They continued to push their way through the wood until they stumbled out of a particularly thick growth and down a small hill to the bank of a gently flowing stream. It was a shallow creek littered with rocks of varying sizes.

Groog and Fred, weary from their hike, knelt down to drink. The water was cool and refreshing. Groog splashed some on his face, pushing his hair out of his eyes.

Behind them, at the base of the hill, was a blackberry bush.

"Lunch," Groog said.

"Indeed," answered Fred.

The two men picked and ate berries, turning occasionally to drink from the stream.

"Psst."

Groog looked a Fred. “Did you say something?”

“No, I don’t think so.”

Groog turned back to the blackberry bush when he heard it again.

“Psst.”

The two friends looked at each other.

“It wasn’t me,” Fred offered before Groog could ask.

“Well, it certainly wasn’t me.”

“Psst. Over here,” a voice from behind them said in a hushed whisper. They turned around and, at the top of the hill, saw the face of a young man hidden in the thicket. “They’re going to see you.”

“Who is going to see us?” asked Fred, standing up.

“Get down!” the young man hissed.

Fred looked at Groog and shrugged.

“Perhaps,” Groog offered, “we should do as he says.”

“Perhaps,” Fred responded, “we should go see who we’re talking to.” He started to make his way up the hill as Groog watched from the bank of the stream.

Neither Groog nor Fred heard the flying pointed stick. They merely saw it strike Fred in the arm. He howled in pain and fell to the ground.

“We got one!” a voice screamed. It was met with a hoot and holler of joy from further down the creek.

Groog crouched low in a panic and looked in all directions. He started to crawl to his friend when an arrow landed in the dirt just to his right.

Fred, writhing on the ground, looked at Groog. “Run,” he said in a choked breath.

And that is just what Groog did. He sprinted up the hill, past Fred, and into the thick growth. He hadn’t gone more than twenty feet when he was tackled. A hand clapped over his mouth, and a voice whispered in his ear. “Quiet. They can’t see us here.”

His heart pounding so hard he thought it might burst through his chest, Groog nodded and rolled over. The boy that had issued the warning leaned over him, a finger to his lips. Not much older than Oog, the boy was malnourished, his ribs visible through his skin.

Groog followed as the boy inched his way toward the edge of the hill, giving them a clear view of Fred. They froze in place when a trio of men approached. Well-fed and muscular, they wore the skins of animals, and carried sharpened sticks, and each had dabs of red on their cheeks and forehead.

One of these men stood over Fred. “Get up.” He kicked Fred in the side. Fred groaned and rose slowly to his feet

“What did I do?” he asked, bewildered.

“Our food.” The man pointed to the blackberry bush. “Our water.” He pointed to the stream. His voice dripped with menace.

“What? I didn’t know.”

“Who else was here?” the man asked.

“No one.”

The man sniffed the air. “Wrong.”

When Fred didn’t respond, the man shook his head and shoved Fred upstream.

Groog tried to fight the instinct to hide from these men and go after Fred, but he was rooted to the spot. “Fred,” he whispered as he watched his friend marched away at the end of a pointed stick, ultimately disappearing from sight.

Groog wheeled on the young man, fury in his voice. “What is going on? What is the meaning of this? Who are those men?”

“This is their territory. No one’s allowed to eat their food, drink their water, or even walk over their land."

The young man seemed hollowed out to Groog, broken. The ire went out of Groog and was replaced by a desperate kind of sadness. "But we didn't know," Groog said.

"They don't care."

Groog shook his head in confusion. "Start again. Who are these people? What is the place? Tell me everything."

30.

After Dag stormed off in search of the leader of the People Who Liked Other People, Oog sat down on a log to think.

It's nice to be liked, he thought. *But why is it nice to be liked? I have not done anything to deserve the affection of these people. Have I? Groog seemed to like me without knowing me, so maybe it doesn't matter?*

But when he thought about it more, he realized Groog had helped him out of kindness and the affection only grew between them as they came to know one another.

"Hey, I like you!" shouted an older woman as she passed by.

"I like you, too," Oog said softly. The two dabbed each other with green paint, and she continued on her way.

That was pleasant, Oog thought, *wasn't it? I mean, it's better than not being liked. Isn't it? Dag was right.* Something about this place felt off, but Oog couldn't quite put his finger on it.

He had been sitting there in confused contemplation for only a few minutes when Dag's voice startled him. "We're out of here." She came stomping toward him, her arms crossed over her chest.

"What happened?" Oog stood up, concerned.

"What happened is that the people in this place are not normal. I want to leave." Her words were clipped, almost fierce.

Oog did not know what to do.

Dag's breathing grew heavy and water started to leak from the corners of her eyes. She touched a hand to the water and started to growl, as if the fact of the tears made her angrier.

Still, Oog did not know what to do. He thought, but nothing came.

Then, on impulse, as if guided by some unthinking part of his brain, he moved forward and pulled Dag toward him. He wrapped his arms around her and made a soft cooing noise.

For a moment, for the barest of instants, Dag stiffened. But then, her body relented, and she melted into Oog's shoulder.

They were standing like that, swaying softly, when Krog approached.

"What's wrong?"

Oog caught his friend's eyes and implored him to ask no more. Krog understood. Gently, Oog led Dag back toward the fence and the edge of the community. Krog followed.

When they passed through the gate, the three of them turned around to look at the small collection of huts, and at the few people in sight, all dabbing one another with splotches of pigment.

The man at the gate was watching them. "Are you leaving?"

"What?" Krog said, surprised. "No, we're not leaving." He turned to Oog and Dag. "We're not leaving, are we?"

Oog looked from Krog, to Dag, to the man at the gate. "I am afraid we must," he said.

"But I love it here," Krog said. "People like me. They really like me."

Oog still had his arm around Dag. "What happened in there?"

"What happened is this." Dag moved her arms and showed a big red splotch of paint just below her collarbone. The man at the gate winced.

Oog and Krog looked at one another in confusion. “I haven’t seen the red dots before,” Krog said. “What do they mean?”

“They mean rejection,” the man at the gate offered. “It means someone doesn’t like you.”

Oog’s upper lip stiffened.

His eyes narrowed.

His back straightened.

“Who did this?” he asked.

“The Great and Powerful Zook,” Dag answered.

The man at the gate winced again. “Ouch,” he offered.

“Who?” Oog asked.

“Their leader.” Dag spat the word leader like it was a bitter root in her mouth.

“Then we must go see this leader. We must make him take it back. Make him replace it with green. Make him—”

“No,” Dag was vehement. “I just want to go.”

“But—” Oog started.

“No buts. I will not stay here a minute longer. Please,” she whispered, “come with me.”

Oog nodded and put his arm around Dag again. They started to move away from the fence, toward the trees. They stopped when they noticed Krog was not following them.

“Krog?” Oog asked.

“I’m sorry. After the People of the Tree, I think I need this place.” His voice was in one measure ashamed and in another desperate.

“Then stay,” Dag said, with bitterness in her voice. “But be careful, Krog. If you’re really searching for answers, you won’t find them among the distraction of a popularity contest. There are no shortcuts in seeking the truth."

"Perhaps," he said, "I need a break from the truth. Perhaps the distraction is the point."

Dag nodded once and turned to go.

Oog stopped, caught between the two; Dag was moving away from the fence, while Krog stood resolutely near it. Krog saw Oog's hesitation and spoke.

"Go, my friend. Go and find your fire and be happy. But come back to this place and visit me."

The two friends embraced. "I can never repay you," Oog said, "for freeing me."

"No," Krog said softly in answer. "It is you who freed me."

Oog nodded, turned, and walked to Dag. He put his arm around her once more, and together they made their way into the woods. The last thing they heard was Krog talking to the man at the fence: "Hey, I really like you!"

31.

Cagu had assembled a small army.

He led a phalanx of nearly twenty People of the Tree, all dressed in the fiercest animal skins—wild boar, wolf, elk with towering antlers—all with their faces painted, and each carrying sharpened sticks and clubs.

"Men," Cagu began.

"There are eighteen of us, sir. Nineteen, if we include you," one of the men interrupted.

"Yes, Pythos. Thank you." Cagu bit back an exasperated sigh. Pythos had a well-known and seemingly unstoppable penchant for counting everything.

"That's thirty-six legs, thirty-eight if we count yours. Fifty-seven if we count everyone's third leg. Were any of us female—"

"Yes, Pythos. We get it. Thank you."

Pythos, realizing his colleagues were staring at him, and not in a kindly way, fell quiet.

"We must be more cautious than our prey," Cagu said. He motioned to the destruction left by the fleeing Oog, Dag, and Krog; thick footprints, trampled plants, broken branches and sticks. An unmistakable path. "March in single file and leave no trace we were here."

One of the men raised his hand. He was another of Cagu's nephews.

"Um...I have to pee," the young man said. "Where can I do that?"

Cagu could not understand why his sister had given birth to such colossally stupid children. "Go off the trail," he said with impatience.

One by one, other hands went up. Cagu pulled on his own hair. "Oh, for the love of Decidua, go, all of you, go."

All but one of the soldiers fled to the woods, half of them holding their private parts as they ran. A chorus of water streaming onto leaves made the Forest alive with sound.

The soldier who remained was a stout and sturdy man. He stood at attention, his eyes fixed forward, a grim look on his face.

"What is your name, brother?" Cagu asked.

"Nero, sir."

"And you, Nero, don't have to pee?" Cagu said the word "pee" with obvious disgust.

"No, sir. I can hold it."

"It's going to be a long march from here, I suspect. The signs of the path are at least a day old."

"I am in service of Conifo and Decidua, sir." He splayed his hands over his head as if he were a tree and twirled once in place.

Cagu had noticed Nero before. He was among the most pious of his people, always early to ceremonies, and always quick to point out others who were not toeing the line. He remembered one incident in which Nero had personally flogged a newcomer who had picked a ripe apple from the branch of its tree. Nero's punishment had made Cagu nervous that his own night raids to pick fresh fruit from trees might be discovered. But the anxiety didn't take root; Cagu knew he could simply invent some new rule of the religion to justify his actions. It really is good, he thought again, to be king.

"Thank you, Nero," he said. "How would you like a larger role in our little army?" Nero's straight line of a mouth tweaked up ever so slightly at the corner.

When the others came back from relieving themselves, Cagu assembled them in a group.

"This is Nero," he said. "He will be my second-in-command." Nero stood up a bit straighter. "Should anything happen to me, should I be detained or incapacitated for any reason, you will follow his instructions. Is that clear?"

"Seventeen third legs drained," Pythos blurted out.

The soldiers rolled their eyes at the observation, mumbled their agreement, and assembled in a loosely configured line that seemed to satisfy Cagu. He was just turning to go when Nero spoke up. Loudly.

"Did you maggots hear our leader?" Everyone stopped and stood still. "Are those half-hearted noises of agreement the best you have to offer?"

One young man gave a tentative, "Sir, no, sir?"

"That's right. Now, who are we?"

The men looked around at one another, at the Forest, at their feet, at the sky.

"My name is Bruce," one man offered tentatively.

"I'm Droogalooga—"

"No!" Nero bellowed, interrupting Droogaloogaloogaloo and frightening the entire unit into stunned silence. "Who are we?"

"The People of the Tree?" Bruce asked.

"Yes! Now, let me hear it with enthusiasm!"

"The People of the Tree!" they cheered.

"Who?" prodded Nero.

"The People of the Tree!" they shouted.

Nero cupped a hand around his ear. "I can't hear you!"

"THE PEOPLE OF THE TREE, SIR!" they yelled as one.

Nero turned to Cagu. "The men are ready to move out, sir."

Cagu's eyebrows arched halfway up his forehead. "Remarkable," he whispered.

"Thank you, sir. I have a knack for keeping things orderly."

"So you do. Very good, Nero. Very good indeed."

With that, Cagu turned and led his men into the wilds of the Forest.

In one short day's march, the warriors found themselves at the fence line of the People Who Liked Other People but Didn't Seem to Like Dag.

The woman sitting on the fence stood as she saw them approach.

"Hi there! I really like you gu—" She never finished her sentence. A pointed stick pierced her chest and stuck in her heart. She fell off the fence, landing on her face.

"Threat neutralized, sir," Nero said to Cagu.

Cagu stared at his lieutenant before opening his mouth to speak, but no words came.

"Yes, sir," Nero said with pride, "it certainly was a perfect kill shot."

"Yes," Cagu drawled in response, "but perhaps next time, let's talk to whomever it is first."

"Of course," Nero said, smacking his forehead at his own impatience. "An interrogation. My apologies, sir."

"Riiiight," Cagu responded. He ordered his men to collect the body and drag it back to the tree line before anyone in the village noticed. There, on Cagu's orders, the small army hid in the trees, watched, and waited.

32.

Fred had left a trail of blood.

Red blotches were smeared across leaves, branches, and the shell of an unfortunate Speeder Snail named Daryl. The blood made Daryl, who had an aversion to all things gruesome, faint, falling with his soft belly exposed. The fainting made him appear dead. Appearing dead did nothing to stop Groog from stepping on Daryl, which made Daryl actually dead.

As for Groog, while the sight of Fred's blood made his stomach turn, at least it made his friend easy to track. Groog moved swiftly through the trees, pushing the limits of his aging muscles, pausing only briefly to scrape what remained of Daryl off the bottom of his calloused foot.

The young man who had tried to save Groog and Fred, who Groog had learned was called Clint, trailed at his heels, struggling to keep up. "We can't just storm in after them," he panted through ragged breaths.

"Why not?" Groog asked over his shoulder, not breaking stride.

"Wait." Clint grabbed Groog's arm to stop him. "Wait."

Groog stopped and turned to face Clint. He found his new young friend doubled over and breathing heavily. "We can't let them get too far ahead," Groog said with growing impatience.

"Listen," Clint said, slowing his breathing. "You don't

understand. These guys are really bad news."

"I should say that's pretty obvious, don't you think?" Groog didn't mean for his words to have such a sharp edge, but the level of distress he was feeling was an entirely new emotion.

Clint ignored Grog's tone and tried a different approach. "Groog, I'm sorry, but your friend is probably already dead." His words, while direct, were delivered with the utmost care. "This group kills without thinking, acts without reason."

Groog looked over his shoulder in the direction Fred had been taken, and then again at Clint as he considered this. He sat down on his haunches to think. Could this boy be right? Was Fred already gone? Should he, Groog, simply return to his original quest to find Oog?

No. Fred was captured because he had left his home to help Groog. Maybe Fred was dead, but maybe he wasn't. Groog couldn't just abandon his new friend. He owed him that.

"I'm sorry, Clint. I can't just turn away. I understand if you don't want to come, but it would be a great help if you did. You know these people and I do not. Plus, two thinkers are always better than one."

With great reluctance, Clint nodded and followed Groog, who had once again picked up the trail left by Fred and his captors.

"What are these people called?" Groog asked as he ran.

"The WeFolk," Clint answered, trembling at the very mention of the name.

33.

As Cagu, Nero, and the other People of the Tree crept low along the edge of the clearing outside the encampment of the People Who Liked Other People but Didn't Seem to Like Dag, Conifo and Decidua moved silently around them. The two ancient tree beings found a spot a few paces from a soldier named Byong, another nephew of Cagu, who had fallen asleep.

Conifo and Decidua extended their roots into the hard soil, settling in to watch what would transpire.

A small rodent with a bushy tail and floppy ears attempted to make a nest in Decidua's lowest branch. The tree god picked the creature up, and put it gently back on the ground, creaking as she did. "Go now, brave soldier, and help your people."

Terrified at the notion of a talking tree, the animal scampered away.

The interaction resulted in a small amount of noise, causing Nero to lift his head.

"Did you hear something?" he asked Cagu in a harsh voice.

"No," his general answered.

And that was that.

NOTES ON LOVE

A middle-aged white man, whose name has been lost to the sea of time, once said, "Love makes the world go 'round."

That is not true. The Earth spins because of the way it was formed. Billions of years ago, a giant cloud of gas, a sort of intergalactic fart, collapsed from its own gravity and started to rotate. From that moment, the planets, including Earth, were born. The Earth continues to spin to this day because there is no opposing force to stop it. In other words, given the absence of sound in space, the Earth is the result of the longest silent-but-deadly in the history of time. So no, love does not make the world go 'round.

Another white man, a sort of poet, once said, "All you need is love."

This is also untrue. Without air, water, and food, people cannot survive. Perhaps they won't want to survive without love, but they can if they try. This white man, who was just shy of being middle-aged, was later shot by a different middle-aged white man, though there was no known connection between the shooting and the line about needing love.

An actual poet—very middle-aged, very white—with a very dark imagination, once said, "We loved with a love that was more than love." This is what scientists call a paradox, which is to say, it is not true. Scientists like to spend many hours at chalkboards trying to prove that paradoxes are true. It turns out they can prove anything if they get the maths right. And when that doesn't work, they invent new maths, which is in itself a paradox.

There was no known connection between this noted poet, Edgar Allan Poe, and a popular entertainer (neither white, nor middle-aged) named Rodney Allen Rippy, who recorded a song called "World of Love" when he was only twelve. It is rumored that both artists would develop a bad case of indigestion when writing about love, producing uncountable numbers of silent but deadly farts.

One person who really understood love was, surprisingly, a crusty middle-aged white man of privilege, who lived in a crusty middle-aged society of privileged people. His name was Alfred Lord Tennyson. (You can see a clue to his privilege right there in his middle name.)

It was Tennyson who said, "'Tis better to have loved and lost than never to have loved at all."

Boom.

It just goes to prove that not all middle-aged white men are total wankers.

Just most of them.

34.

The wind had picked up and the weather had continued to grow colder. For warmth, Oog and Dag found themselves walking close enough to be touching, their hips and shoulders occasionally brushing.

Dag was developing powerful and unfamiliar feelings for Oog. She caught herself stealing glimpses at the lines of his arms and legs, especially his arms. She liked the curled mop of hair on his head and how, when it caught the sun, it was the same color as the earth after it rained. But most of all, she was drawn into his eyes. There was curiosity and wonder in those eyes and it made her wish she could see the world through them.

Dag, whose heart was beating a bit faster, and whose breath was coming a bit shorter, decided to make conversation to distract herself.

"Is it cold where you live?" she asked.

"No," he said. "You?"

"No," she answered.

On hearing this, Oog stopped and sniffed the air. "If it's warmer where you live and it's growing colder as we're walking, then maybe we're going in the wrong direction?"

Dag stopped and looked around. Her shoulders slumped. Oog's

observation about the weather reminded Dag how thoroughly lost she was. "I don't know," she half-groaned, half-whispered. She wrapped her arms around her torso, trying to get warm.

Dag wished Oog would hug her again, to ward off the cold, to make her feel better, but she didn't know if she could ask this of him. Could she? Or maybe she could just hug him? The thought of doing so made Dag nervous, so she hugged herself tighter, which made her feel even worse.

Little did Dag know that Oog also very much wanted to hug her again. But Oog was fairly certain there existed an unspoken rule about doing such a thing. Groog had once explained about the unspoken, unseen rules of the Forest.

"Rules?" Oog had asked. "Like never try to touch the fire?"

After growing increasingly comfortable with fire, Oog had tried to pet it. He learned that the fire did not enjoy affection of any sort; just more fuel.

"No, that is, or should be, an obvious rule," Groog had answered with patience. "I'm speaking of less obvious rules that are generally unspoken."

"Such as?"

Groog proceeded to rattle off a long list of dos and don'ts. Do make room for an elder on the log, even if it means you have to stand up. Don't pick nits off someone without asking them first. Do dip your hands in the stream after doing your business. Don't do your business in the stream. The list went on, but Groog never covered any unspoken rules related to females.

"Perhaps," Oog suggested now, hoping he could do something, no matter how small, to brighten Dag's spirits, "we can find something to block the wind." He surveyed the landscape. "There," he said, pointing at a large oak. "The wind is blowing toward the tree. Maybe it will be less cold on the other side."

Dag looked up and let a weak smile play across her face. "You really are a good thinker, aren't you?"

Oog felt his cheeks flush in spite of the frigid air. On seeing this, Dag's smile grew stronger; she took his hand and led him to the tree. She felt bold and empowered by the action, which, along with the touch of Oog's warm hand, let a glimmer of happiness find its way into her heart. "There are really no young people in your village?" she asked, wanting to continue the conversation, wanting to hear his voice.

Oog, caught off guard by Dag's hand in his, missed the question. "I'm sorry, what?"

"Your village."

"Yes, I come from a village."

Dag laughed. "Yes, tell me about the village."

"There are no young people there." This caused Dag to laugh louder, which caused Oog to panic. The stiff breeze notwithstanding, a bead of sweat formed in the space between Oog's nose and his upper lip. "What?" he asked in complaint.

"That's exactly what I was asking you about."

"You were?"

"Yes!"

"Oh. I'm sorry. I guess my mind wandered." Oog looked down at their intertwined hands and then up at Dag.

"I guess so," she said; it was almost a whisper.

They arrived at the oak. It was a sturdy tree with just enough room for the two of them to sit huddled together on the leeward side.

"Hey," Dag said, "it works! This isn't quite as cold." She leaned harder into Oog, pressing her head into his shoulder. "So, your village?" she asked again.

"Yes," Oog said. "I come from a village."

Dag stifled a laugh. "Why are there no young people?"

"I don't know. It was something of a controversy to allow me to join the group when I did. Some of them didn't want me at all."

"But the man you spoke of..."

"Groog."

"Yes, Groog. He did?"

"Yes. And so did Mother."

"I thought you didn't know your mother."

"She was not my mother, nor the mother of anyone who lived there. But she was older and wiser than the rest, so everyone just called her Mother."

"Fascinating."

"What about your village? Are there young people?"

"Oh yes, many. From the smallest children to those my age."

"Are they all thinkers?"

Dag paused, taking a deep breath, and slipped her arm through Oog's. She squeezed tight, and he returned the gesture.

"This is nice," she said.

"Yes." The word was more of a croak. Oog wondered if physical contact made a person lose his voice. He wished he could ask Groog.

"By the time someone is our age," Dag said, "if they have not developed the ability to think, they are driven away. It's a very sad day for the village. The non-thinkers don't understand what they have done wrong. They will try to re-enter the village for a day or two, but they are denied food and shelter and love, so eventually they leave."

Oog stared at Dag, his mouth agape. “That’s awful.” Dag nodded but didn’t respond. “Why not let them stay, and, I don’t know, care for them?”

“The elders say non-thinkers are dangerous, that they are animals, not people.”

“Is that what you think?”

“No,” Dag answered softly. “It’s why I left. I was looking for my friend, Girl. She was a non-thinker.”

Oog didn’t know what to say, so he said nothing.

“I tried to change the minds of the villagers, but no one would listen. ‘This is how things have always been, Dag,’ they told me.” She heaved a heavy sigh. “I suppose it is how they always will be.”

“And yet you want to return.” Oog offered this more as an observation than a question.

“It’s my home.” Dag’s answer was tinged with sadness and regret, but also longing and finality.

“Some days I wish I was still a non-thinker,” Oog said.

“You can’t mean that.”

“But I do.”

“Then, you shouldn’t say it out loud.”

“But it’s true.”

“Sometimes even truths can be a dangerous thing.”

“The truth is the only thing that can never be dangerous.”

“Did you learn that from Groog?”

“Yes.”

Dag nodded. “We have a word for people like Groog in our part of the Forest.” Oog waited for her to continue. “Idealists.”

“What does that mean?”

“It means they hold their ideals so sacred they cannot see reason.”

Oog thought about this, letting the notion roll around his rapidly growing brain. Something about it didn't seem right. "Give me an example of when the truth would be a bad thing."

"The man who didn't like me and put the red blotch of paint on my body. What was to be gained by that man sharing that truth?"

"But that wasn't truth."

"It wasn't?"

"It was opinion masquerading as truth."

"Another Groogism?"

"Actually, no," Oog answered with pride, "I just made that one up myself." Dag smiled and huddled closer. "I believe what Groog told me. There is nothing more important than the truth."

They were silent for a while. They continued to huddle close, using the tree to divert the wind, and using each other's bodies to generate heat.

"Then tell me the truth, Oog," Dag said, a hint of mischief in her voice. "What do you think of me?"

Oog's eyes went wide; his stomach and lower intestine each shriveled to a third their normal size and tried to switch places. "Uh..."

Dag laughed.

"Uh..."

"Exactly," she answered. "And by the way, I feel the same." Her face flushed with warmth as she said these words out loud. She feared maybe she'd gone too far, been too direct. Oog was about to respond when Dag cut him off. "Anyway, we need to find food and water."

Grateful for, and aghast at, the change in subject, Oog nodded agreement. "Yes...food...water," he managed to mutter.

The two about-to-be-more-than-friends, still holding one another, stood up, left the shelter of the tree, and continued on.

35.

It had been two days since Oog and Dag had left the People Who Liked Other People but Didn't Seem to Like Dag, and already Krog missed his friends. While he enjoyed the good feeling and camaraderie of his new acquaintances in the village, Dag's parting words, about popularity contests and the truth, had taken root in his mind.

These people were very nice, and it felt good to be liked, but they didn't really do anything. Krog asked who had built the huts and the fence, and no one seemed to know. "Ask Bilga," one of them finally offered. "He's been here the longest. Maybe he remembers. And hey, I really like you!" Krog was dabbed with green paint. He gave a half-hearted smile and dabbed the person back without speaking.

The more inquiries he made, the more Krog heard the name Bilga. There was no agreement on where the man actually lived, and no two descriptions of him were the same. It was almost as if this Bilga was a character from a myth or legend.

Intrigued, Krog searched high and low. His hunt led him outside the fence, and finally, after several hours of looking, he found a well-constructed and well-hidden hut in a copse of trees. It was a squat, sturdy building with a closed door for walking through, and smaller closed doors set into the walls, which Krog imagined were used for looking through.

"Hello?" he bellowed.

"Don't move," a voice whispered behind him as a pointed rock was pressed against the small of his back. "And be quiet."

"What?" Krog whispered.

"What do you want? Why are you here?"

"I mean you no harm. I only have questions."

"Turn around. Slowly."

Krog did as instructed and found himself face-to-face with a shriveled old man. Less face-to-face, actually, and more face-to-chest, for the man was very small. "I seek Bilga," Krog said.

The man looked left and right and sniffed the air. He nodded. "Come inside. Something is skulking in the Forest today. Something other than you, I mean."

Krog was about to protest, but the man had already gone through the door of the hut. Not knowing what else to do, Krog followed him.

The interior was a large room with a dirt floor and a pile of straw in one corner. Once the door was closed, it was almost completely dark.

"Is there no way to let light in? Can't you open those small doors in the middle of the walls?"

"They're called windows, and of course I can, but as I told you, something is out there and we must be cautious. Now, who are you?"

"My name is Krog, and I am new to the village. Do I have the honor of speaking to Bilga?"

"I am Bilga, and we are speaking, but I think you should reserve your opinion about whether or not it's an honor. Now, sit down." Bilga hunched down on the ground and Krog followed suit. "Why have you sought me out?"

Krog found the man's intensity and manner of speech off-putting. "I have questions?" he asked, his voice tentative and confused.

"I should warn you, if you're going to ask if I like you, I'm going to bonk you on the head." Bilga's countenance, already defensive and paranoid, now bordered on hostile.

"I'm sorry?" Krog was profoundly bewildered.

"Ever since that idiot took control of the village and people started liking one another, they seem to put a premium on getting me to like them back. But let me tell you young man, the last fool who tried to put green pigment on my—"

"I'm not here to like you," Krog said, cutting him off. "I'm here to find out who built the fence and the huts."

Bilga's eyes narrowed. Krog couldn't see this because it was dark, but the old man's eyes narrowed just the same. "Why?"

"Because, I am new to the village, and I wish to learn its history."

"No one wants to learn the history."

"I do."

"Again," Bilga said, "why?"

Krog saw no reason to hide the truth. "Well, these people, they spend their time so concerned with liking one another, I don't see how anything of value ever gets done."

Bilga sat back. His eyes had adjusted to the dark, the scant light coming through the cracks around the doors and windows providing just enough illumination for him to see the earnest look on Krog's face. "Really?" he asked. "This isn't some sort of trick?"

"Trick?"

"He didn't send you?"

"Who's he?"

Bilga was silent for a long moment, considering everything that had been said, when finally, he let out one large exclamation: "Ha!" He slapped Krog's knee for good measure. "You have given me hope, young man. I thought the world had completely lost its mind. But if you're here, there must be more like you out there. Tell me, where do you come from?"

"The village of my birth is very far from here. I left many moons ago in search of answers. I want to know the meaning of life, what happens when we die."

"And what have you found?" Bilga leaned forward, keenly interested in Krog's answer.

Krog thought on this. He ruminated on his time with the People of the Tree, and he considered what he had seen so far of the People Who Liked Other People but Didn't Seem to Like Dag. "I have found," he said, leaning forward, "that people are crazy. Well, all except for two..."

At that instant, there was the clear sound of someone's voice whispering on the other side of the door. Krog recognized it instantly as the language of the People of the Tree. They had found him.

"I'm not sure what it is, sir," the muffled voice said, "but it appears to be some sort of cave made of sacred trees. Shall we destroy it?"

"We must go," Krog said in an urgent whisper.

Bilga nodded. He stood and walked to a small pile of rocks that sat next to the bed of straw. He took one, hefting it in his hand, considering the weight. "This will do," he said, breathing more than speaking the words. Bilga then approached the window on the wall opposite the door. He opened it a crack and peered out, then opened it wider. He turned to Krog. "Be ready to run."

Krog nodded.

"Hey, you grass-eating fart heads!" Bilga shouted out the window. "Over here!"

There was a commotion outside as a stampede of feet ran around the house to the source of Bilga's shout. One face after another filled the window. Krog recognized all of them, including Cagu. Bilga reared his arm back and let the rock fly, smashing one of the faces, an older man named Caius, on the bridge of his nose.

"Ow!" Caius yelled and went down. The others tripped over one another backpedaling.

"Now!" Bilga yelled. And he and Krog fled through the door.

NOTES ON POWER

Among the most intelligent species in the Forest was a small rodent with a bushy tail and floppy ears that looked like a larger, more cunning version of a squirrel. In the language of Oog, they were known simply as Fat Squirrels; in their own tongue, they were called Twizzlevarmint.

For millennia, the Twizzlevarmint lived a peaceful, agrarian existence. They gathered nuts, burrowed nests in the trunks of trees, and used rudimentary tools, including the wheel and even fire. A Twizzlevarmint liked nothing more than riding through the Forest on a unicycle while noshing on roasted chestnuts.

The very first queen of the Twizzlevarmint, for they were matriarchal in nature, ascended to the throne five thousand years earlier. Her name was Leilani, which translated as Leilani; she was a benevolent ruler who cared deeply for her subjects. Her progeny followed her example, and for many of centuries, the Twizzlevarmint lived a golden age the lengths and likes of which had never before been known and has not been seen since.

But generations of inbreeding caught up with the Twizzlevarmint. Fifty years before the age of Oog, a queen named Glorianus the Grotesque—her name a strong clue as to the kind of leader she might turn out to be—changed everything. She instituted rules that forbade unicycle riding on certain days of the week, required each citizen to pay a chestnut tax that left families without enough to feed their children, and created a cult of personality forcing common folk to worship her as a god.

One school of Twizzlevarmint historians posthumously diagnosed Glorianus the Grotesque as a paranoid schizophrenic with a narcissist complex. Most of the other schools labeled her as an asshole.

Glorianus raised her children and grandchildren to rule with the same iron paw, beginning a decades-long era of repression. The path of least resistance being a seductive mistress, the people, or in this case the Twizzlevarmint, endured many years of hardship.

Then, a Twizzlevarmint neuromathematician—a branch of mathematics unique to their species—conclusively proved that power corrupts and absolute power corrupts absolutely. A corollary of this proof was that repression, when expressed as a binary sum of unhappiness and pain, will always lead to revolt. A group of Twizzlevarmint high school students seized on this and thus began the Twizzlevarmint Civil War.

The height of the Twizzlevarmint Civil War was taking place just as Oog and Dag were leaving the land of the People Who Liked Other People but Didn't Seem to Like Dag, and just as Groog was laying eyes on tyrants of another sort.

36.

Groog and Clint lay flat on their stomachs. They were a hundred paces from the edge of an encampment.

"Is this your village?" Groog asked in a hushed voice.

"No. That's actually pretty far from here. This is an outpost the guards use to patrol a very wide perimeter surrounding the village. They do it to keep outsiders out, and villagers in."

The camp was composed of things Clint called "tents." They were small shelters fashioned from animal skins, stitched together, and propped up with tree limbs. They were arranged in a loose circle. On the ground, at their center, was Fred.

His arms were tied behind his back, and his feet were bound. Dried blood caked the spot on his bicep where he had been speared. His head was down as if he was asleep, but Groog could tell from the shaking of his shoulders that Fred was crying.

Milling about, not paying much attention to Fred, was a group of guards—Groog counted fifteen—dressed in the same manner as those who had taken Fred. They wore animal skins and had red liquid smeared on their faces.

"I thought you said they were called the Wee Folk?" Groog asked.

"They are."

"Well, they don't look very small. In fact, most of them look quite big."

"Not wee-folk. WeFolk." Clint made a circular motion with his hands, taking in everything and everyone around him.

Groog looked back at the WeFolk trying to parse Clint's meaning, when he noticed a familiar face. It was the person who had attacked his village. Only now, the little man's face was smeared with red, and he wore the hide of a bear.

"I know that one," Groog whispered, pointing at No Name. "He's the non-thinker who attacked our camp. Or at least I thought he was a non-thinker."

"Ssshhh," Clint said. "Look."

Three people, two men and one woman, emerged from one of the tents. One man was taller than the other, and Groog, not knowing their names, thought of them as Tall Man, Short Man, and the Woman. The rest of the group stopped what they were doing and gathered round. The scene had the air of something important taking place.

"Are those the leaders?" Groog whispered.

"There isn't really a leader," Clint answered. "Well, not officially."

"What?"

"Watch...it will all make sense soon. Sort of." Groog glanced at Clint, then back again at the unfolding scene.

The two men and one woman—none of the three were old, but none were young either—walked in a circle around Fred. When one stopped, the other two followed suit. It almost seemed a game to Groog; each one taking turns stopping, trying to force the other two out of step. But it never worked. They moved in perfect synchronicity.

The trio stopped circling, and Tall Man spoke.

"We have done well to bring us a captive." Two of the guards beamed with pride. "Thank we."

"Thank we?" Groog asked Clint.

Clint put a finger to his lips and nodded for Groog to continue observing.

Tall Man knelt down to get eye level with Fred. “How do we answer for our crimes?”

Fred looked up and scrunched his eyes. “What?”

“How do we answer for our crimes?” Tall Man said again, this time in a more pointed way.

“How in the Forest should I know how you answer for your crimes?”

There were gasps all around, one person uttering, “Blasphemy.”

“What?” Fred’s fear and confusion were brewing into anger and frustration.

“We are an outsider,” Short Man said to Tall Man, “and have not yet sought or received enlightenment. It might be that we simply don’t know.”

“Ignorance of the law is no excuse,” the Woman countered. “We cannot tolerate it.”

Groog thought he was starting to understand. “WeFolk?” he whispered, emphasizing the “we.”

“Yes,” Clint whispered back. “They are a pluralistic collective. They believe they have one unified mind.”

Groog paused to consider this. “Does that work? Do they actually think and act as one?”

Clint, a nervous and twitchy boy who rarely made eye contact, looked directly at Groog. “Not at all.”

Short Man, who had tried to soften the mood and come to Fred’s defense, responded with, “Now, when we say we, do we mean we,” he made a motion taking in the entire group, “or do we mean we?” and he pointed at Tall Man.

“They spend more time,” Clint whispered, “arguing about how to collectively think than actually accomplishing anything useful. It's a nightmare."

"Be careful," Tall Man said. "When we single out one, we diminish the whole. Besides," he added, "our ignorance may be a ruse. We might be infiltrating the land as a precursor to invasion. This outpost exists specifically to guard against such threats."

"I've heard enough," Fred said, rising to his knees. "I demand you untie me."

Groog, aching to help his friend, started to rise on instinct. Clint held a firm grip on Groog's wrist, and the two tussled for a moment, making a small noise.

"There," the Woman said, wheeling in their direction and pointing. "More of us! It is an invasion! Go, now, find us and bring us back to..." She fumbled for a second at her own confusing sentence. "...us. Bring us back to us!"

"Um," one of the guards said, choosing his words carefully, "we mean that we," he motioned to another guard, "should bring us," he pointed to the bramble where Groog and Clint had been hiding, "back to us?" He motioned at the Woman and her two male companions, being careful not to point at any of them individually.

"Yes! Go!"

The momentary lack of clarity gave Groog and Clint a head start, and they were off. Less than a hundred paces from where they started, they found a ditch on the far side of a large, old tree. They ducked in and remained very still as they heard the guards pass them. They lay there for a long time, as quiet and motionless as possible.

Groog finally broke the silence. "I don't understand. They think as a collective, but they are singling Fred out for his crimes?"

Clint nodded. "The WeFolk are riddled with contradictions. They punish anyone they consider to be a transgressor, yet they capture and assimilate new thinkers."

"Is that what happened to you?"

"I was rounded up with a group of new thinkers, so I played dumb and went along until I saw an opening and escaped."

"And those three people, the two men and the woman, they run the show?"

"Really, it's the tall guy. Everyone else is afraid of him. One time he—"

Clint was interrupted by Fred's screams. The tortured sound echoed off the trees, filling the Forest with terror. Only two words could be distinguished from his cries of despair.

"Groooooooooog! Ooooooooog!"

There was a final yell of pain and anguish, and then silence. Groog knew in his heart of hearts that Fred was dead.

"Now," Clint said, "we must go now."

This time Groog didn't argue.

37.

Bilga's surprise attack with the rock through the back window of his hut had shocked the People of the Tree. They were so discombobulated by the sudden appearance of not only the rock, but of the window itself, that they fell back, giving Krog and Bilga a head start out the front door.

Knowing this part of the Forest as well as he did, Bilga darted around trees, over fallen logs, and across one small tributary of the larger river. Krog stayed close behind.

At the edge of the clearing, with the fence line in sight, they saw the woman assigned to guard the entrance lying in a pool of her own blood, a pointed stick protruding from her chest.

"Oh my," Bilga panted, stopping to look.

"Ibi!" came a shout from behind them. Nero, his fist in the air, led Cagu's army and began a charge toward Bilga and Krog.

"Quickly," Krog said, "we must close the fence."

"Right," Bilga agreed.

They crossed the clearing, stopping to pull the ropes affixed to the inside of the gate, closing it behind them as they entered the village.

The fence was seven feet tall and was one of the more marvelous feats of engineering constructed in all the Forest. It was made of cut logs bound together with vines and mud and enclosed one thousand paces of space in each direction. It had cutouts every one hundred paces for guards to stand watch, though every single one of the cutouts was currently empty.

As soon as the gate was closed, a middle-aged man strode up to Krog and Bilga. "Hey!" he said. Both men, gasping for breath and looking frantic, turned to face him. The newcomer didn't seem to notice their distress. "I like you!" He reached forward with green paint on his finger.

Bilga slapped the man's hand away.

"Hey!"

"The village is under attack, you imbecile."

"That's still no reason to be mean."

"Did you hear me?" Bilga screamed. "We're about to be killed!"

"You hurt my feelings," the man snarled, poking Bilga in the chest with each word, and then strode off.

"Oh, for the love of...c'mon," Bilga said to Krog. "Let's go."

"Where? All these people are the same. They're brain-dead."

"Not the leader."

Behind them, at the fence line, they heard the banging of rocks against the outer wall. Krog looked back in fear before tramping after Bilga into the heart of the compound.

They passed groups of people dabbing each other with paint, sitting and eating fruit, and picking nits and scratching butts. Krog couldn't help but notice the entire village seemed to be reverting to some sort of non-thinking state. It was as if the endless popularity contest had created a pall of stupidity that hung over the people and infected their brains.

When Krog and Bilga reached the leader's hut, two guards outside the door stood at attention. Having been reprimanded for letting Dag pass two days earlier, they had been instructed to take a different approach with visitors.

"Hey man," the first guard said, "I really like—"

"Shut up." Bilga didn't break stride.

"Whoa, whoa, old timer. Where do you think you're going?" The younger and larger guard backpedaled, blocking Bilga's way. The other guard also sprang to action, and the two made a formidable defense.

"Out of my way. I need to see Zook."

"The Great and Powerful Zook isn't receiving visitors just now," the first guard said.

"But know that he likes you," added the second guard with a smile.

"Listen," Bilga said.

"Yeah?" the second guard asked.

"No, liiiiisten..." Bilga drew the word out, as if he thought the guards were colossally stupid, which he did. He even cupped his hand to his ear for added effect.

By this time, the ruckus at the front gate could be heard through the entire village. Shouts and screams of terror had joined the sounds of rocks and sticks hitting the outside walls.

The guards looked at one another, each cocking an ear toward the commotion.

"What's that?" the first guard asked.

"Marauders at the gate," Bilga said calmly. "Now, you can either let us in, or we can wait here together until they knock down the fence and come for Zook themselves."

"Maybe we should wake him," the first guard said to the second.

"I don't know. The Great and Powerful Zook is pretty keen on his naps."

Bilga's temper flared. "Keen on his na—?"

"Look," Krog said, stepping forward with a smile. "I really like you guys." He dabbed his finger in the first guard's bucket of paint and touched it to each man's shoulder. Each guard visibly exhaled on receiving the validation. "And see, I know these guys outside the fence. They're bad news. They don't like anyone, not even each other."

"Whoa," one of the guards whispered. "Not cool."

"If we can't get in to see the Great and Powerful Zook," Krog continued, "none of us will be able to like anyone ever again. In fact, that's what these guys want. They are the People Who Like to Stop People from Liking One Another."

"Really?"

"Really."

"Dang. Okay, you'd better go in."

"And you'd better get to the gate," Bilga said. "They're going to need all the help they can get."

With that, the two guards, who had once again failed to guard their leader, ran off toward the fence line. On the way, Krog saw them stop to like a passing friend with a dab of green paint.

"Well played," Bilga said.

"You can thank me later. Right now, let's wake up this Zook fellow and find a way out of this mess."

"Right."

And with that, the two new friends entered the hut.

38.

Oog and Dag walked two more days after leaving the shelter of the oak tree. They linked arms often for warmth, slept with their bodies pressed close at night, and foraged for water and food together. And, most of all, they talked.

They talked about the sun and fire; they talked about their adventures together and apart; and they spoke of their villages and friends. With each passing step, the two grew closer in body, mind, and spirit. Oog felt more connected to Dag than anyone other than Groog, and maybe even more so than that.

On the third day, they came to a sharp drop in the land that fed into a lush canyon. A thick roof of faded yellow leaves on the treetops made it impossible to see what was below.

"It looks like a sea of floating hummingbirds," Oog offered. Dag nodded and gripped him tighter. It was beautiful, but opaque, and the uncertainty of what lay below made them nervous.

Oog and Dag talked about trying to bypass the ravine, to find a way around, but Dag picked up the scent of water, and they were thirsty. Very thirsty. Together, they made their way down the hill, letting gravity pull them from tree trunk to tree trunk. When they reached the bottom, they each turned slowly in every direction, taking in their surroundings. What lay before them took their collective breath away.

Stretching out along the trough of the canyon was a burbling stream of clear water flowing over smooth, rounded rocks. On either bank of the stream were wildflowers in an assortment of colors—purples, magentas, teals, tangerines—leading up to trees with ash white trunks and yellow leaves. Impenetrable from above, the leaves were translucent from below, letting a filtered sunlight bathe the entire scene in a shimmering gold.

"Wow," Oog offered.

"You can say that again," Dag responded.

"Wow," Oog offered a second time. They dipped their faces to the stream and began to drink.

"Hey," a voice called from far away, "over here!"

Oog and Dag both jerked up and saw a person, seeming small at this distance, waving their arms and motioning for them to come.

Oog's instinct was to run. In his experience, encountering people usually ended with him getting bonked on the head. Or worse.

Dag touched his arm. "We need food and rest. Maybe they can help."

Oog looked at Dag and saw exhaustion in her eyes, weariness in the way she held her shoulders. He drew in a deep breath and nodded. "Okay, but let's be cautious." Dag hooked his arm, and together they went down the stream, toward the voice.

The person beckoning them forward turned out to be a young woman, not much older than Dag. She wore no animal skin, though she had clearly used some sharp implement to shorten the length of her hair.

"Hey!" she greeted Oog and Dag with warmth.

"Hello," Dag answered with caution.

"My name is Trish."

"Trish," Oog sounded out the word.

"Yes," Trish said more slowly and carefully. "Trish."

"Trish," Oog repeated her slow rendering of the word for no other reason than to fill the silence.

"Look," Trish said to Dag, "is he okay?"

Dag rolled her eyes. "I'm Dag and this is Oog. Can you tell us where we are?"

Relieved that the two newcomers were both thinkers and fluent in her language, Trish's shoulders relaxed. "Welcome to Town. I hope you don't mind me calling you over, but we don't get many visitors."

"What kind of town is this?" Oog's tone was guarded.

"What do you mean?"

"I mean, do you worship trees? Do you like other people?"

Trish looked at Dag in confusion. "Really, is he all right?"

Dag stifled a laugh and smiled. "Yes, he's fine. We've just had a rough go of it the last few days."

"Well then, please come and share our food and drink and tell us all about it."

39.

The Great and Powerful Zook lay a-snooze in his bed.

Snoring.

Loudly.

Krog marveled at the bed. Small wood posts lifted stitched animal skins off the ground. *I bet that keeps him warmer,* Krog thought. *I have to tell Oog about this.*

Bilga kicked the bed. Hard. So hard he jostled the buckets of green and red paint on the floor nearby.

The Great and Powerful Zook sat bolt upright, disoriented. "I like you!" he exclaimed with the particular brand of confusion that comes with having a dream interrupted. And the Great and Powerful Zook's dream was a doozy. He had been floating on his back in a secluded pool of the river, the sun making the water around him sparkle. A beautiful woman fed him grapes. To have been pulled away from that dream seemed criminal. But the Great and Powerful Zook was still too disoriented to do much about it. "No more grapes?" he asked.

"Wake up, Zook," Bilga said.

"Dad?"

"Yes, dad."

Krog's gaze shot from one to the other. He could see it. Bilga must have looked like this when he was younger, only shorter. Krog could barely contain his surprise.

"Leave me alone."

"Shut up, son. We're in trouble."

Blinking his eyes, Zook seemed to notice Krog for the first time.

"Who's this?"

"I'm Krog."

"Go away, Krog. You don't have an audience with the Great and Powerful—"

Bilga reached down and used his strength to upend the bed, dumping the now Less-than-Great-and-Perhaps-not-so-Powerful Zook to the ground. "Listen to me you colossal disappointment of a nitwit, the village is under attack."

This news caused Zook to pause long enough to hear the screams and howls of dismay coming from the front gate. "Attack?"

"Yes," Krog said. "It's the People of the Tree."

"Who?"

"Look," Bilga said exasperated, "it doesn't matter who they are. They are trying to break down the fence. We need to rally the people to stand and fight."

For the first time since waking up, Zook smiled. "Fight? Oh, father, you really are old-fashioned. We simply need to like them. They will like us back."

"And just how are you going to like someone who is ramming a pointed stick through your chest?"

Zook shook his head and got to his feet. "Listen, Dad, have you ever seen a more harmonious place to live than this? I know you didn't understand at first, but by now you have to see how well this is working. Everyone is happy. These Tree People are thinkers, right?"

"Yes," Krog said.

"Then they'll understand. They won't be able to help themselves."

For a moment, Krog wavered. Being liked was very seductive. But then he thought of the empty guard posts along the wall, the broken doors on two of the huts he passed, and the growing piles of refuse left out in the open. "No," he said.

"No?" Zook simultaneously furrowed his brow and smirked.

"I was once a Person of the Tree," Krog continued. "They believe in something bigger than popularity. Something incredibly stupid, but bigger. Simply liking them will not slow them down, it will not protect your people. The only thing that will protect your people is a leader to rally them to self-defense."

"Look, kid, I think I know more about leading than you. We simply have to—"

Zook's words were cut off when Bilga picked up the bucket of red paint and dumped it on his son.

Zook screamed in agony, as if the bucket contained scalding water. "What...what...what have you done? You. Crazy. Old. Man!"

"C'mon," Bilga said to Krog. "Let's get out of here."

Krog looked at Zook, shrugged, and followed his friend out the door.

The scene outside Zook's hut was chaos. The screams from the fence line were growing louder and were now accompanied by the groaning of wood as the People of the Tree tried to knock down the gate. A variety of villagers, covered with varying amounts of green paint, were running to and fro with no apparent destination.

"Stop!" Krog shouted.

Those in the immediate vicinity, not realizing how desperate they were for leadership, came to a halt and gathered closer.

"You just came from the Great and Powerful Zook," one of them said. "What did he say?"

At that precise moment, the Great and Powerful Zook emerged from his hut, disheveled, wild-eyed, and covered in red paint. Several of the people around Krog and Bilga screamed in horror, and one fainted.

One of the people who had not fainted pointed a finger at Zook and bellowed, "Unpopular!" He picked up dirt and threw it at Zook. Quickly, the others followed suit. The mob filled the vacuum of leadership that had been plaguing the People Who Liked Other People but Didn't Seem to Like Dag. Zook retreated into his hut. The rabble were about to follow when Krog screamed again. "Stop!"

And again, they listened.

"We can worry about The Great and Powerful Zook later. Right now, we need to band together to repel these invaders. Our lives depend on it."

The groans of wood at the gate turned to loud cracking, popping sounds as the logs split, and the screams intensified.

"What do you want us to do?" one of the people asked.

"Here's what I'm thinking." Just as Krog was about to begin, he felt a dab of paint on his back. It was Bilga.

"I like you kid, what can I say?" He laughed out loud.

With that, everyone huddled close to hear Krog's plan.

40.

When the army of the WeFolk broke camp and marched through the woods, No Name marveled at their precision. They stepped in unison, making it appear as if they were one large, living organism, and yet they moved with almost no noise.

How much more could I accomplish if I had an army of thinkers? he thought. *I have been wasting my time with glorified monkeys.*

This army, No Name understood, was pursuing the two people who had been hiding in the bushes. Even with the raspberry smeared on his face, he had still been able smell them. Why had these strange people been oblivious to the scent? Was there some connection between thinking and a dulling of the senses? Yes, that had to be the case. It was why the old people seemed so helpless and feeble.

What he didn't understand was why, after these raspberry-faced people killed the man from the wooden cave, it took them so long to begin their pursuit. They spent more time making gibberish noises at each other than actually doing anything.

Fred's death hadn't bothered No Name—he had taken lives before—but he wondered what it meant for his own safety. Could he just leave these people if he wanted? He didn't think so. Why else would they have put the fox-bag over his head and forced him to march through the woods? No, a new paradigm was unfolding, one in which he, No Name, was the hapless captive. He was now the beetle caught in the spider's web. The realization almost made No Name turn and run. But something stopped him. Something he had not felt in a long time:

Fear.

He did not like it. He did not like it at all.

Perhaps some of these other people are like me. Perhaps they, too, were captured. Maybe they're also frightened, he thought. Some of them certainly looked frightened. And, more to the point, they smelled frightened.

As No Name walked in time with the rest of the army, his mind wandered. *I will steal guards from these raspberry-faced people to raise an army of my own. A new army, made up entirely of thinkers. And then I will have fire, and I will rule the Forest.*

Lost in his reverie, No Name's steps fell out of sync with the rest of the army. One of the Raspberry People from the front of the line came back to yell at No Name. He didn't understand the words, though he grokked their meaning.

Realigning his march, No Name realized his first task must be to find a way to communicate. Building an army of non-thinkers required only non-verbal communication. Snaring and controlling thinkers was a new task and it required a new skill.

He turned to the man walking at his flank. "Globba globa, gluba," he said.

The man looked at him with an eyebrow raised, then glanced nervously forward. No Name and the man were at the back of the pack, and no one appeared to have heard No Name's question. The man's shoulders relaxed. "I'm sorry, what?" he whispered.

"Bladogadoto demour." No Name, understanding there must be a reason to keep their voices low, whispered as well. He attempted to smile, though it was more of a scowl than an expression of happiness. He tapped his own chest and made another unintelligible sound.

The man thought maybe he understood, so he pointed at himself. "Bob," he said clearly and slowly. "Wait, no," he corrected himself. "I mean We. I am We. I mean, We are We." He shook his head in frustration.

No Name, who had listened very carefully, repeated back the only word he managed to salvage from the man's short rant. "Buh-ohb."

The man lit up, though he once more stole a glance to the front of the line. Again, no one could hear, or at least no one seemed interested in their conversation. "Yes. That is, or was, my name." All the tension went out of him. "It's such a relief to hear it again. Thank you." He put a gentle hand on No Name's shoulder.

No Name didn't understand the words, but he knew they were said with friendship and encouragement. As they continued to march, No Name used hand signals to ask Buh-ohb to teach him more words. In short order he had learned "tree," and "sky," and several different words for food.

No Name smiled to himself, a genuine smile this time. The pieces of the puzzle were falling into place. He continued to move forward in the synchronized march of the army of the WeFolk, scheming, and dreaming, as he always did, of fire.

NOTES ON HARMONY

Many millennia after the time of Oog, an Englishman will write a book about a group of boys stranded on an island with no adults. In the story, the boys devolve into warring factions and a savage-like existence. Decades of students, assigned this book by decades of language arts teachers, will scoff at the tale.

"The adults are projecting their own failings on us," the students will privately think. "If kids were stranded on a desert island, we'd figure it out."

In the year 2067, they will get their chance.

A variant of a normally benign virus, called the Omega Variant, will kill everyone over the age of fourteen on Long Beach Island, New Jersey, in the span of two days. By a turn of colossally bad luck, this mutated pathogen will strike just as a category four hurricane—Hurricane Ralph—is assaulting the small barrier island. The causeway connecting the island to the mainland will be destroyed, and all power to the small community will be lost, plunging the survivors into darkness.

A rescue boat will reach the island three days later. Stunned emergency workers will find all of the children gathered in a school, eating healthy meals, reading books by candlelight and flashlight, and discussing rational systems of government they might form should rescue never come. The story will be reported by most major media outlets, but it will gain no traction for the shame adults feel when hearing it.

Four of the island's children, each of whom will grow up to become a language arts teacher, will lead a campaign to ban the offending book from school curricula forever. The effort will fail, proving that the only thing that corrupts more than absolute power is absolute adulthood.

41.

Dag and Oog sat on a log and warmed themselves by a fire.

Fire!

Dag could not believe their luck. Oog's search was over. She would accompany him back to his people, the ones he called Groog and Mother, with the fire, and then together they would search for Dag's village. Maybe if she told her people about all she'd experienced, they would see the folly of their ways and things would change.

Like the people of Dag's and Oog's villages, the Townsfolk, which was how they referred to themselves, did not know how to create fire, only how to tame and preserve it. Oog spent most of the afternoon talking with their fire keeper, an older woman named Sica. She was tall and thin, with wavy hair all over her body, and a warm, inviting laugh. Dag spent her time shadowing Sica's daughter, the village leader, a remarkable young woman named Em.

"How is it that such a young person is the leader here?" Dag asked. "In our villages, elders are the leaders."

Em smiled and nodded. "The practice dates back to before anyone can remember. But it seems to work well, so it is our way."

"Are you the ruler for life?"

"Oh, no. If we allow one person to lead for too long, we believe that person has the capacity to become drunk with power." There was a loud chattering from the trees as a group of passing Twizzlevarmint rebels cheered the sentiment. Dag ignored the noise and thought about what Em was saying. If young people ruled her village, then maybe Girl and the others would have been allowed to stay.

"So," Dag asked as she thought more about it, "you will not always be the leader?"

"No," Em said warmly. "I have six revolutions of the constellations. Then I will join the council of elders and a new leader will be chosen."

"Council of elders?"

"I rely on advice and need consent for my actions from a council of elders. This group always includes the most recent leader, but also many other members of the village, especially those who have lived long and fruitful lives. In this way, with a young leader guided by a small group of older people, we balance wisdom with ingenuity, caution with boldness."

By that evening, Oog and Dag had been welcomed to the family of Town. The assemblage of people, a larger population than either Oog's or Dag's village, was a diverse group of older and younger, male and female, thinkers and non-thinkers. They sat around the fire eating berries, nuts, and fruits, and sharing stories. The non-thinkers, not understanding the words, lounged by the fire, lulled by the sound of the voices and the love of those around them.

Together, Oog and Dag told the story of the People of the Tree, and of the People Who Liked Other People but Didn't Seem to Like Dag. The Townsfolk hung on every word. When Dag told of their escape from the People of the Tree, there were audible gasps.

That night, as they lay side by side, warmed by a small satellite fire lit just for the two of them, Dag and Oog whispered to one another.

"I like this place," Dag said. "A lot."

"Me, too," Oog answered.

"Can we live here? If they'll have us, I mean."

Oog reached over and took Dag's hand. "Nothing would make me happier. But I still must bring fire back to my village."

Dag squeezed his hand. "Of course, my love, of course." This was the first time Dag had used the word love, and it hung in the air like the moon.

Oog turned his head to face Dag. She could feel his breath mingling with her own. Without knowing why, she gently pressed her mouth against his. Oog pressed back.

Much later, the two of them fell into the most contented sleep of the

42.

Just as Krog and Bilga were arriving at the battered front gate to the village of the People Who Liked Other People but Didn't Seem to Like Dag, the fence crashed inward. As the dust and splinters of wood settled, Cagu, Nero, and the army of the People of the Tree stood with rocks in their hands and bloodlust in their eyes.

Behind Krog and Bilga stood an opposing force of humans, their skin stained green, all holding rocks of their own. Even the Formerly Great and Powerful Zook, his skin a mix of green and red—and where those colors overlapped, a disgusting shade of brown, not unlike excrement—had joined the throng.

"Vos dedere!" Cagu shouted through the splintered opening in the fence.

"What manner of speech is that?" Bilga asked Krog.

"It is the language of the People of the Tree," Krog said. "He wants us to surrender."

The People Who Liked Other People but Didn't Seem to Like Dag muttered in confusion as Krog's explanation spread through the crowd.

"There's more than one language?" someone asked.

"They can talk to trees?" one person at the back yelled.

"Yes," responded another. "Either that or they are trees."

"They don't look like trees."

"And trees don't look like people," the Formerly Great and Powerful Zook stated with confidence. "But hey, I like trees!" Those standing next to him took a few steps away, creating a barrier of empty space.

Krog ignored them all, squared his shoulders, turned to face his former comrades, and shouted, "Numquam!"

"What does that mean?" Bilga asked.

"Never," Krog said.

"Oh, right. Good one!"

"We will kill every last man, woman, and child here," blurted Nero in the language of the People of the Tree. Cagu glanced at him sideways and the other men shifted uncomfortably. Seeing this, Nero's shoulders sagged. "Too much?" he asked Cagu.

"Maybe a bit, for the start."

Krog, not wanting to scare his army, did not translate. Instead, he shouted back, "There are more of us than there are of you!"

"We are better armed," answered Cagu.

"We have resources here."

"We can return with more."

With this repartee being conducted in a strange tongue, Krog's people—the ones who liked each other, but not Dag—did not understand what was being said and quickly grew bored. Those standing farthest back began to wander off, or would have, had not something remarkable begun to happen behind the People of the Tree.

The Forest, it seemed, was coming to life.

Not in the sense that it was teeming with life, which it was, but in the sense that two large trees—one with large, green leaves, and one with pine needles and pinecones—had uprooted themselves and were slowly making their way across the clearing to take up a position behind Cagu and his men.

The soldiers closest to the edge of the woods, sensing something behind them, turned to see the very trees they worshipped as gods. One by one, every last member of Cagu's army dropped to the ground and lay prostrate.

Krog, who had a clear view of this, muttered, "Well, I'll be a Fat Squirrel's uncle." His jaw went as slack as a non-thinker. Terrified beyond all reason, the rest of the People Who Liked Other People but Didn't Seem to Like Dag fled, hiding around corners of huts, stealing glances when they could muster the courage. Only Bilga and the Formerly Great and Powerful Zook remained standing with Krog, but even they took an instinctive step back.

"Ha!" Nero, who was oblivious to the goings-on behind him, spat. "You see? Your people quake in fear before our army. Victory is ours."

"Surrender now, Krog," Cagu, also oblivious to the movement of the trees, said, "and we will have mercy in meting out your punishment. In the name of Conifo and Decidua..." Cagu's voice trailed off as he was interrupted by a loud, low rumbling, as if the Earth were clearing some phlegm from its throat. Slowly, he and Nero turned around.

"You were saying?" boomed one of the trees.

Nero fainted.

Cagu said, "Oh shit," which needed no translation. He, too, dropped to the ground.

NOTES ON CURSING

As we have seen with Oog and No Name, when the very first thinkers encountered one another, they had no way to communicate. While they could grunt and growl, those sounds were insufficient for the rich life presented by their newfound powers of thought. Necessity being the mother of invention, these proto-thinkers created language.

The very first word was, not surprisingly, "hungry."

The next four words, spoken in response to the first word, and also not surprisingly, were "please don't eat me." (While linguistic historians argue that the first complete phrase ever spoken could not have possibly included a contraction, facts are facts. Even when they're made up.)

What was surprising was the fifth word.

The person who had said "hungry," not understanding the response of "please don't eat me," shrugged her shoulders and walked away. When she took her first step, her foot came down on the rock-hard shell of a Speeder Snail. The unexpected pain caused a twisted noise to shoot out of her mouth which sounded something like "Fuck!"

"What did you say?"

The hungry woman turned around. "You heard me." The preponderance of new words was coming fast and furious now.

The Speeder Snail, whose name was Rusty, shook his head, retreated into his shell, and muttered "humans," to himself, with no small amount of disdain.

"Fuck? What does that even mean?"

"It means 'ouch,' just worse."

"Well, don't say it again. I don't like it."

And so, the very first conversation between human beings also contained the very first act of censorship. Like most acts of censorship, it failed miserably, and people have been saying "fuck" in one form or another ever since.

43.

You see," boomed the tree with the pine needles, "while we're not actually gods, we rather liked being worshipped."

"Quite," said the tree with leaves.

Cagu and Nero had joined their colleagues lying face down on the ground and shaking. Krog, Bilga, and the Formerly Great and Powerful Zook stood in frozen amazement.

"But when this, this..." The first tree pointed a branch at Cagu, unable to find just the right word.

"Twizzlevarmint, dear?" offered the second.

"Yes, my love, that is just what he's like, a little creature that scurries in our branches and causes us irritation. Spot on. When this Twizzlevarmint started hurting people in our names, enough was enough."

"D-Do you mean to say...?" An astonished Krog nodded meekly at the tree with the pine needles. "Y-you are the actual Conifo?" Then, he motioned to the tree with leaves. "And Decidua?"

"At your service," Conifo replied. The voice was deep, sonorous, and deliberate.

For a moment, Krog was too startled to speak. He had spent two years trying to make his heart and mind believe Cagu's stories about these trees, that they were all-powerful beings who demanded his fealty. But in two years he had seen no evidence they existed, nothing to suggest they were anything more than an invention of Cagu's imagination. Meeting Oog and seeing his treatment at the hands of Cagu had been the final straw. For the past few days, since escaping from the People of the Tree, Krog had felt liberated.

Only now, here they were. The very gods whose existence he'd finally had the courage to deny were looming over him.

Krog was more than a little confused.

"I'm more than a little confused," he said.

"About what, dear?" Decidua asked.

"If you were speaking to Cagu, and he was your agent among men to ensure our service to, and worship of, you, why did you let him carry on the way he did for so long?"

"We have never before spoken to Cagu," Decidua answered. "And as we have taken great pains to keep our existence a secret, we're not quite sure how he even knew who we were."

"Yes," Conifo said, drawing out the word. "Do tell us, Cagu, how do you know who we are? We're all ears."

"We don't have ears, dear."

"It's an expression, love."

"Ah."

Cagu, whose shaking had crescendoed into full-blown quivering, stammered, "L-l-l-lucky g-g-guess?"

"You see?" Decidua said, turning to her mate. "I told you."

"Yes, my love, you did."

"I'm sorry, what?" Krog asked.

"We had a wager. I had 'lucky guess,'" Decidua said.

The Forest went completely silent.

"What?" Krog asked again.

"Lucky guess," Conifo answered in a calm, deliberate voice.

"You're saying, and I want to make sure I have this absolutely right," Krog started, trying to collect his thoughts, "you're saying Cagu invented the entire story about you, and that it just happened to turn out to be true?"

"We have been alive more revolutions of the heavens than all of you combined," Conifo answered, waving a branch over Cagu's army, sweeping it farther to include Krog, Bilga, the Formerly Great and Powerful Zook, and even farther to acknowledge the faces of the People Who Liked Other People but Didn't Seem to Like Dag peeking from around the corners of huts. "In that time, we have come to discover something important about the basic underlying nature of the universe. The very thing, actually, that fuels daily life and makes the world go 'round."

A few of the People of the Tree raised their eyes and craned their necks forward. Like Krog, they had been in search of answers and had taken Cagu at his word. Now, they felt they were about to get some real answers. Krog leaned forward, too.

"Yes?" he asked.

"What's it saying?" Bilga whispered.

"HE is saying," Decidua answered, shifting to Bilga's language and underscoring Conifo's preferred pronoun, "that everything that happens in this world is fueled by one irrefutable cosmic law."

"Love?" Krog guessed.

"Curiosity?" Bilga ventured.

"Lucky guesses?" Cagu said into the ground.

"No," Decidua said. "Coincidence."

"Coincidence," Conifo repeated the word in the language of the People of the Tree.

"Coincidence?" Krog asked, incredulous. "You're saying, and

again, I want to make sure I have this right, the answer to life, the Forest, and everything, is coincidence?"

"Well, you haven't really asked a question, dear, but in short, yes. Everything that happens, is really just happenstance."

"I even once worked out the maths," Conifo said, "but as my calculations were scratched into dirt, they didn't survive the first rain."

Krog shook his head as if he was trying to dislodge water from his inner ear and was about to ask more when Nero stood up.

"Wait, wait, wait," Nero said. "Are you saying that everything he told us," he pointed to Cagu, still on the ground lying next to where Nero stood, "was a lie?"

"Well, he did get our names right. And we are, you know, trees. But everything else, yes, that was false."

"And the Great Tree? That was not a man you turned into a tree for his folly?"

Decidua chuckled. It was like the sound of branches rattling in a heavy wind. "That was one of our favorite stories, but no. It's just a tree. A very lovely tree, but a tree."

"Does it walk and talk like you?"

"Not that we've ever seen, dear, but you never know."

"So," Nero's voice was at the midpoint on a continuum between anguish and anger, "I speared and killed the woman sitting outside the entrance to this very village for no reason at all? It was not in your service?"

"I never told you to do that!" Cagu shouted, lifting his head for the first time.

"We are peaceful beings," Conifo said. "We do not kill, and we would never ask another to kill in our name."

Nero let out a tortured scream and kicked Cagu. "Get up, dog!"

The other People of the Tree started to rise as well, forming a circle around Cagu as they did.

"No," said Conifo in a thunderous yet somehow gentle voice that commanded attention. Everyone froze and looked at him. "Another thing you learn when you have enough time is that two wrongs will never make a right. We cannot let you harm Cagu." Conifo reached forward with a branch and plucked Cagu out of the center of the throng.

"Thank you, my lord, I—"

"Quiet," Conifo boomed again. "Do not thank me. Do not speak. Your life is spared, but your association with others is at an end. You must leave this place and never return." He put Cagu down behind him, away from the other People of the Tree.

"And while we're at it," Decidua said, taking two large strides forward and speaking in the language of the People Who Liked Other People but Didn't Seem to Like Dag, "you must also leave." She reached forward and picked up the Formerly Great and Powerful Zook.

"Hey," he said in the smoothest voice one could muster when being picked up by a walking, talking tree, which is to say not smooth at all, and used a finger to remove some green paint from his neck and touched it to Decidua's branch, "I like you."

Decidua half-sighed, half-laughed. "No one cares, dear."

"No one at all," added Conifo in the same tongue.

"In our short time here," Decidua said, "we have seen how you have sapped the life and spirit from these people for your own self-aggrandizement. You must also leave and never return."

Decidua set the Formerly-Great-and-Powerful-and-Now-

Utterly-Banished Zook down next to Cagu.

"Please, my lords," Bilga said, stepping forward, "he is my son. Can you not find it in your hearts—?"

"We are not lords," Conifo interrupted, "and we do not have hearts as you understand them. But this is as much for your son's safety as it is a punishment." He used a branch to point behind where Bilga and Krog stood. The People Who Liked Other People but Didn't Seem to Like Dag had started to come out from behind their huts; they had hatred and murder in their eyes.

"But, but..." Bilga looked pleadingly at the People Who Liked Other People but Didn't Seem to Like Dag. He was about to protest, to remind them they were accountable for their own actions, that they had willingly followed the Formerly-Great-and-Powerful-and-Now-Utterly-Banished Zook, but in his heart, he knew it was a futile effort. A mob was a mob and could never be reasoned with. He let out a long, slow sigh and turned to Krog. "I must go with him."

"What? No!" Krog exclaimed. "You're needed here. We can't rebuild without you."

"You can and you will."

"He's a grown man, he can fend for himself."

They both looked to Zook, who was at the moment dabbing Cagu with green paint and saying, "Hey, I like you!"

"He's an idiot," Bilga said, "but he's still my son."

Not sure what else to say, Krog nodded.

Bilga strode forward to stand next to Zook and Cagu. "C'mon, boys. Time to go." The two disgraced former leaders hung their heads and followed their elder across the clearing and into the woods.

"Well, then," Decidua said, "I think our work here is done." She and Conifo turned and started to go.

“Wait!” shouted Krog. “What do we do now?”

“Do?” Conifo asked. “Do whatever you like. That’s the thing about thinking beings, you have free will. Exercise it.”

“But if you want some advice,” Decidua added, “I think your other friends, the boy and the girl, might need some help. Strange things are afoot in the Forest. Most unsettling.”

“Come, love,” Conifo said. And with that, Conifo and Decidua intertwined their branches, and walked into the woods and out of this story.

44.

The following morning, Oog and Dag were up early, ready to depart. Sica prepared a burning log for Oog to carry back to his people.

"This will last most of the day, but not beyond that. By nightfall, it will be spent. You must stop every few hours to find dry wood and transfer the flame."

Oog nodded and took the log with great care and reverence. "I can never thank you enough," he told Sica. "All of you," he added, looking around.

Most of the Townsfolk had come out to see Oog and Dag off on their journey. They formed a semicircle around their two new friends, the opening in the circle pointing to the exit from Town.

"Our thanks will be your return," Em said in reply to Oog.

Dag hooked her arm through Oog's. "We will," she said, and then looked at Oog.

"We will," he added, "and if it's all right, we may bring some friends."

"Friends of yours are friends of ours. All are welcome here," Sica said. She then stood face-to-face with Oog and bent forward to touch her forehead to his. She did the same to Dag. Sica then took a step back and lowered her gaze. Everyone else in Town lowered their gazes as well.

Oog and Dag didn't know it, but they had just been recipients of the highest and most intimate honor a member of Town could bestow on another person: the famed Town Head Touch.

Thousands of years hence, when much of the world population was ravaged by a forehead-borne virus, the descendants of the original inhabitants of Town were immune. As their connection to the famed Town Head Touch was lost to the sea of time, those immune were thought to be an evolutionary step forward for humanity. Which, if you think about it, they were.

The scene as Oog and Dag prepared to leave grew so quiet one could have heard a Speeder Snail run. Somberly, but with a swelling feeling of love, Oog and Dag took the silence as their cue, and with their heads held high, walked out of Town, each hoping it would not be for the last time.

45.

Oog and Dag climbed back out of the valley, Oog holding the burning log as if it were a sacred artifact. As they crested the same hill they had first descended, a light rain—a drizzle—started to fall.

"Let's follow a course that keeps us under as much cover as possible," Oog said.

Dag scanned the floor of the forest around them and found a fallen branch that was still thick with leaves. She picked it up and held it over Oog's log, creating a small, traveling roof. "Will this help?"

"Brilliant," Oog murmured and leaned over to kiss her on the top of the head.

It was in this manner—Oog holding the log, Dag protecting it from the drizzle—that they made their way slowly forward. Only, they didn't know where they were slowly going.

"Um," Oog said, coming to a stop, the valley far enough behind them that it was no longer visible, "before we found Town, did we come from that way?"

Dag looked in each direction and bit her lip. "I don't really know."

"Neither do I," Oog sighed.

"Wait," Dag said, letting her makeshift umbrella fall for a second, "what's that?" She was pointing at a small clearing on their left.

"A small clearing?" Oog asked, confused.

"Yes, but look at the grass in the clearing."

The drizzle, which had now become a mizzle, was making the floor of the clearing glisten with fine droplets of rain. All, that is, except for one wide path directly across the middle. The grass had been trodden, and recently.

"I see," Oog said.

They followed the path across the clearing, Dag taking pains to keep the fire as protected from the mizzle as possible.

"And look here," she said, pointing at the ground where the grass gave way to the forest floor. The earth was growing soft and muddy as the precipitation continued to grow in intensity. "These are footprints. It appears whoever came through here was going that way." Dag nodded deeper into the woods. Oog crouched down for a better look and Dag joined him.

And this is how they were, both squatting low, when they heard a shout of "NO!" from just behind them. Oog turned just in time to see the large stick coming down to bonk him on the head.

Seriously? he thought, just before he blacked out.

NOTES ON COINCIDENCE

The most famous coincidence in human history involved Sir Isaac Newton, an apple, and the discovery of gravity.

None of it was true.

First, Newton was hit with a pear, not an apple.

Second, he wasn't sitting under an apple (or pear) tree. He was sitting on a bench on the grounds of Cambridge University, eating a buttered roll for lunch.

Third, the apple (pear) didn't fall from a tree. Rather, it was hurled at Newton from a second story window by a graduate student named Tom Gilegane, an Irishman with a penchant for mischief. Gilegane had told his friends earlier that morning of his intent to "plaster" Newton because, according to Gilegane, Newton was a "sodding wanker." This was an opinion shared by many but voiced by few.

And fourth and finally, gravity was not discovered any more than Newton's fellow countrymen "discovered" distant lands. Both gravity and those lands had been there all along. And like those lands, which had been inhabited by millions of souls, gravity was pretty sure it had made itself reasonably well known to all it encountered.

In fact, the only coincidence in the entire affair occurred when the exaggerated follow-through of Gilegane's throw caused him to lean too far out his window and into the open and waiting arms of gravity. He fell, or more accurately, was pulled to his untimely death. Gravity is said to have been satisfied, because it thought Gilegane was a "sodding wanker."

46.

Oog was dreaming.

Again.

He was lying on a bed of hay held together with vines, only the bed was high in a tree. His face was being pelted by small droplets of rain, which were strangely warm. He turned his head and looked down over the edge of the bed to the woods below.

He saw himself and Dag facing off with two shadowy figures. The burning log he had been carrying lay smoldering at his feet.

Oog wanted, needed, to climb down, to jump down, to fly down and protect Dag. The shadowy figures signified danger; he knew it in the deepest part of his being. He needed to act, and act now. Only he couldn't. When he looked down toward his feet, he saw he was bound across the legs and torso. He struggled to free himself, but it was no use. He tried to scream, but that was no use either.

In fact, his screams, which he thought had no sound, had an echo of laughter.

Laughter? he thought.

Yes. The Forest echoed with laughter.

The sound of it floated up and enveloped him. It carried Oog, bed and all, up past the trees, through the clouds, and into the darkness beyond. It carried him all the way back to consciousness.

Oog opened his eyes.

Dag was standing nearby, and it was she who was laughing. She was talking to a thin young man about the same age as Oog, and he was laughing, too. Then, Oog felt a hand on his forehead. It was rough and old, but tender. His nostrils were flooded with a familiar smell. It was the smell of home.

Oog sat bolt upright and whirled around, which made his head spin. But he didn't care. "Groog!" he exclaimed.

His friend and mentor sat beside him, a smile plastered from ear-to-ear, water in his eyes.

"I believe this is how we first met," Groog said. And he and Oog fell into a long, tight, and glorious embrace, the two of them joining Dag and Clint in laughter.

Oog, Dag, Groog, and Clint shared the stories of how they had all come to be in this place, the adventures they'd had, the trials and tribulations they'd endured. Even how and why Clint had mistaken Oog for one of the WeFolk and bonked him on the head.

"I am sorry about the fire," Groog said, motioning to the log at their feet, the last wisps of smoke rising lazily into the air.

Oog, whose head hurt, but whose heart did not, patted his elder on the knee. "It's okay. We know how to get back to Town, and I'm certain they will give us more."

"Wonderful," Groog said. "Mother and the others will be so relieved. And proud. You did it, Oog. You completed your quest."

"Almost," Oog answered. "We shouldn't count our Speeder Snails before they've been trampled." Groog raised an eyebrow. "We still have to return the fire to our people, and if these last few days have taught me anything, it is to expect the unexpected."

"Yes," "Indeed," "So very true," Clint, Groog, and Dag said in turn.

"If we leave now," Oog said, "we can make it to Town before dark, spend the night, and leave with fire in the morning."

"Not yet," Groog said.

"Not yet?" Oog was confused.

Dag lay a hand on his arm. "The story they shared," she said to Oog. "The WeFolk."

"Yes, of course." Oog had recoiled at the part of the story where Fred was killed. He was also surprised to hear that the non-thinker who attempted to steal their fire was actually a thinker, and one of these WeFolk.

"We believe they are tracking us," Groog said, "and are not far behind. If we leave for this Town now, we might lead the WeFolk directly there."

"So what do we do?" Oog asked, rubbing the spot where he'd been bonked on the head.

"Clint and I should keep moving. Maybe we can lose them. Then, we can all meet up back at Mother's."

Oog didn't want to become separated from Groog a second time. He looked at Dag, hope in his heart and a question in his eyes. Dag was again lost in those eyes. It made her stomach flutter, like she'd swallowed a butterfly.

Without communicating, the two agreed on a course of action. Dag marveled at this, that she and Oog could communicate without any sort of speech or even a hand gesture. Her parents were the only other people with whom she shared such a bond. She wondered if Oog and Groog had something similar. The thought made her happy, and she hoped they did.

"We will go with you," Oog said, verbalizing their unspoken agreement. She moved closer and linked arms with him.

“Good, good,” Groog answered. The relief he felt was visible in the way his muscles relaxed. “Though we must leave now, and we must go with stealth.” He stood up. “Are you sure you’re ready for this?”

“We are,” Oog said, “but wait just a moment.” He searched until he found a sharp stone, using it to make a mark on a nearby tree, pointing to another tree. On that tree he made a similar mark. He did this four more times. “The path,” he explained to the others, “back to Town.”

“Genius,” Groog said, and put his arm around his adopted son’s shoulders. “Just genius.”

Buoyed by companionship and love, the four friends set off hoping to outrun their pursuers, and to return to Groog and Oog’s home with the fire that would save their people.

47.

An hour after breaking camp, the four friends came on a trail that led directly to a large wooden fence.

"Is this the People Who Liked Other People?" Oog asked Dag.

"No, look at the logs. These are vertical. The logs in the fence around that encampment were horizontal." Oog nodded at the astute observation.

There did not seem to be a way through the fence. There was no door, no window, no ladder to scale the wall, and it seemed to go on without end in both directions. Groog shrugged his shoulders, turned left, thinking this was just as good as turning right, and led the group in search of something useful.

They followed the barrier for what seemed an eternity. It curved slightly as they went, leading them in what they guessed to be a very large circle. After an untold number of paces, they came to a clearing and what appeared to be a sealed gate built into the wall. A well-worn road led from the gate, across the clearing, and into the woods. *This,* Oog thought, *must be the main entrance.* Only there were no people.

"Look," Clint said. He pointed to a vine that hung next to the gate. The other end of the vine disappeared over the top of the fence. A small piece of wood with strange symbols etched onto it hung next to the rope. It looked like this:

Pull the Rope to Ring the Bell

“Does anyone know what those pictures mean?” Groog asked the three of them.

“Nope.”

“Nuh-uh.”

“Not a clue.”

The four of them stood there looking at each other, looking at the wall, and looking at the rope.

“Maybe we’re supposed to use it to climb over the wall,” Oog suggested.

“I don’t know,” Clint answered, “it’s pretty high. Besides, walls are bad things.”

“They keep predators out,” Groog said.

“And they keep captives in,” Clint countered.

“Let’s see if we can find who the rope belongs to,” Groog said. “Besides, we should warn the people who live here about the WeFolk. If we don’t like what we find, we can leave.”

Oog and Dag nodded. Clint shook his head, muttering a resigned, “okay,” under his breath.

“Maybe we need to announce ourselves,” Dag offered.

“Good idea,” Oog agreed. “Hello!” he bellowed.

Nothing.

“HELLO!” he tried in his loudest voice and used his fist to bang on the fence.

Still nothing.

All four of them shouted and banged together. “Hello!” “Is anyone in there?" "We've come to help you!" "Can you open—?"

A face peered over the top of the fence and scowled at them. "Can't you read?" the person shouted, pointing at the sign.

"What is 'read?' " Oog asked.

"Oh, for the love of..." the scowling face muttered to no one in particular. "It is a sign," the scowler said, speaking very slowly. "It has words that explain things to you."

"Words? That we speak? In drawings?"

"Uuuughhh. New Thinkers," the scowling face said under its breath, but loud enough for all to hear. "Yes. They are like pictures, but they are words. Each group of little pictures represents a word you speak."

"Fascinating," Groog said.

"Yes," answered the scowling face, which was now an eye-rolling face, "fascinating." Then the eye-rolling face started to retreat.

"Wait!" Dag screamed. "What do the words on this sign say?"

"It says pull the rope to ring the bell!" And with that, the face disappeared.

Oog, Dag, Groog, and Clint looked at one another. Oog shrugged and pulled the rope. When he did, a loud gong sounded from the other side of the fence.

The scowling face returned, only now it was smiling. "Yes, how can I help you?"

Knocked a little off his game, Groog, who had assumed the mantle of the group's leader, stammered a bit before he answered. "Uh, um, yes. My name is Groog and we'd like to see the head of your...your...?"

"This is The Village."

"We'd like to see the leader of your The Village," Groog said, now with more confidence.

"Sorry, no." The formerly scowling-and-eye-rolling-but-now-smiling face disappeared back over the top of the fence.

"Perhaps we should just go," Clint said.

"No. We must warn them." Groog was determined.

"Must we? They don't really seem like they want to be warned."

"Well, then, let's at least warn this one person." Groog pulled the rope again, this time much harder, making the gong resonate louder.

The face, having returned to its original scowling state, came back. "Look, I've had just about enough of you lot. If you don't—"

"An army approaches," Groog said. "They mean to lay waste to your Village."

"Are you threatening us, Mr. Groog?"

"It's just Groog, and no. We are trying to help you."

"What kind of army?" the face asked.

"A brutal army that kills indiscriminately," Groog answered.

"An army that will not relent until your The Village is vanquished," Clint added.

"How big an army?" the face asked. "I mean, this is a pretty big fence. It's doing a good job of keeping you out."

"Let's just go," Clint said. "We tried."

"They number at least one hundred," Groog answered the fence man.

Color drained from the scowling face, and it once again disappeared behind the top of the wall.

"A hundred? The WeFolk weren't more than twenty," Clint said.

"He doesn't know that."

"A lie?"

"An exaggeration."

A creaking sound pierced the air and hurt their ears as the gate started to rise.

The man from the top of the fence—older and smaller than he had initially seemed—stood in the opening. "You'd better come inside."

48.

The Village was large. Larger than Town, larger than the community of the People of the Tree, even larger than the encampment of the People Who Liked Other People but Didn't Seem to Like Dag.

It was really big.

The man from the front gate led Oog and his friends along a broad avenue lined by buildings. Taken in its entirety, The Village was a marvel of engineering ingenuity.

Each building had wooden doors and windows. One building was made entirely of stones stacked one on top of the other, seemingly held in place with a kind of dried mud. The broad avenue met intersecting trails that went off to the left and right, each lined with more buildings.

Atop some of these buildings were more of what the man at the gate had called "signs." Oog pointed to a large rectangular placard with a drawing of one stick prying another off the ground. Under the picture were the symbols the gate-man had referred to as words. "What does that sign say?" Oog asked.

The gate-man hurriedly glanced over his shoulder, as if an army of a hundred marauders were going to come pouring over the fence at any moment. "It says, 'How have you lived without a lever? Visit Mo's Lever Shop today.'"

"And that one?" Oog pointed at a sign with a thick round piece of wood.

"'We've got deals on wheels. Bruce's Wheel Shop.'"

"And that one?" Oog's fascination was like that of a small child.

The tone of the gate-man's voice suggested he was growing weary of the questioning. "'Get your kicks with sharpened sticks.' Look, let's just get where we're going, okay?" Again, he looked back toward the gate.

And then, Oog saw it.

Another sign.

A glorious sign.

He touched Groog's shoulder and nodded toward it. The two friends looked at one another.

"I'm sorry," Groog said, sensitive to the gate-man's exasperation. "Just one more. What does that say?" He pointed to a sign with a picture of fire.

The man let a long, petulant breath escape his lips. "It says, 'Fire. You need it today. The Fire Shop. Coming Soon.' Now, are we done?"

"Yes, quite," Groog said, smiling at Oog.

The gate-man led the four friends the rest of the way in silence. They arrived at the end of the boulevard where a small park of grass and shrubs fronted a tall building, at least twice the height of all the others. A path lined with multicolored rocks led to double front doors, which were shut and guarded by a large man with a sharpened stick.

"Wait here," the gate-man said, and disappeared inside the building.

"Something doesn't feel right about this place," Dag offered after the man had gone.

"The buildings are impressive," Oog said.

"Maybe," Dag said. "But it almost feels like the only reason they're here is to be impressive."

"What do you mean?"

Before Dag could respond, the gate-man returned. "A will see you now."

"A what?" Oog asked.

"Just A."

"Just a what?" Oog's confusion deepened. He was about to ask more questions when Groog laid a hand on his shoulder.

"Let's ask our questions inside."

The friends looked at one another and entered the building, the double doors closing behind them.

NOTES ON MONEY

The most powerful force on the planet Earth is love. Despite reports to the contrary, all you need is love, and love does in fact make the world go 'round.

Love is such a powerful force that it imbues a rudimentary kind of sentience on everything it touches. Aside from the obvious impact love has on all creatures great and small, it has also left its mark on the trees, the oceans, the earth, and the wind. But perhaps most remarkable was the effect love had on money.

Over time, the planet had become overrun with thin, rectangular slips of paper emblazoned with august faces and numbers, along with round metal discs decorated in the same way. These items, known collectively as money, were so widely fondled, caressed, and coveted that, through the power of love, they became self-aware.

The papers and discs passed from hand to hand, from pocket to pocket, from large fortified building to large fortified building, basking in the warm glow of their adoring public. The way people loved the paper and discs seemed to be unconditional. Nestled in their wallets, stacked in their vaults, crumpled under mattresses, the money felt perfect contentment.

But then, something unexpected happened.

Human beings began to use computers—at first the size of small buildings, later the size of small wristwatches—to transfer the pieces of paper and metal discs to one another. With people no longer needing to touch money, love migrated to the glowing screens of the computers. The emblazoned papers and metal discs were forgotten, and eventually abandoned.

Left to their own devices, trillions of these forgotten souls stewed in their new misery. "We have been forsaken," they said to one another. "The horror. The horror."

As nearly immortal beings, the emblazoned paper and metal discs were in no hurry. They spent centuries formulating a plan to recapture their former glory. And so began the Great Currency Revolt of 2754. Millions of lives were lost on six planets in a war that lasted nearly a decade. In the end, the papers and discs were destroyed, which, it was said, caused the glowing screens no small amount of smug satisfaction.

49.

The inside of the building was unlike anything Oog and his friends had seen before. The ground wasn't dirt, but rather, an artificial floor made from the wood of trees. The planks weren't rough like the logs that made up the outside of the buildings; they lay flat and smooth. Scattered about were animal skin rugs—deer, elk, bear—on which sat small pedestals.

"What are those?" Oog asked, pointing at one.

"Chairs." their guide said, a note of deep resignation in his voice at having to deal with the relentless barrage of questions. "They are for sitting."

More remarkable than what lay on the floor was what stood before them.

A blocky, boxy, indoor hill rose to an upper level of the building. This, too, was made from the wood of trees. It was a series of small platforms, each one also made smooth. The entire group stopped and stared. Cliff sniffed the air.

The gate-man rolled his eyes. "They're stairs. You walk up them. To get to the second floor of the house."

"Second floor?" Groog asked.

"How do they not fall down?" Oog added quietly, almost reverentially.

"Magic," the gate-man said with all the acid he could muster. "Look, if there is really a marauding army about to invade, perhaps we'd better get on with this, yes?"

Groog nodded and the gate-man led them up the stairs.

The weight of the group made the stairs groan and creak with plaintive agony, like it was crying for release. Oog grasped Dag's hand in fear.

For all their ingenuity, the People of The Village, or, The Village People as they were known, hadn't yet refined the art of metallurgy beyond the creation of their gate gong. As such, the stairs, walls, ceilings, and floors of the building were held together not with screws and nails, but with a special kind of mud mined from a mostly dry riverbed located a two-hour walk away. It gave one the feeling that the entire structure was going to fall down at any moment. Which it probably was. Oog, Dag, Groog, and Clint, knowing none of this, were terrified and awestruck just the same.

At the top of the stairs, they found themselves in a large room. At one end was a chair which was placed in front of a wooden table. Sitting in the chair was a man. He was looking at a piece of very thin wood that was covered with the little pictures the gate-man had called words. He rose to greet them.

He was tall and lanky and wore animal skins more closely fitted to his body than anyone in their group had previously seen. And these skins seemed to be painted with long vertical stripes running top to bottom.

"Sir, these are the people who claim to have seen an approaching army."

"Thank you." The man said this in a way that made it clear the gate-man was being dismissed. On his way out, the gate-man stopped in front of the group and waved his arms. "It's air," he said, "you breathe it." Satisfied with this final insult, he made his way down the stairs, muttering "morons," as he went.

"You'll have to forgive Felipe. He's not well-suited to his job, but he's the only one willing to do it. My name is A; please, sit." He motioned to a collection of animal skins on the floor. The group squatted down as A sat back in his chair.

"It is a pleasure to meet you A Please Sit," Groog began.

"No. It's just A. The leader of The Village is always known simply as 'A.'"

Groog cleared his throat and craned his neck up to look at the man. "I am Groog. This is Oog, Dag, and Clint." He pointed to each of his friends.

"Welcome to The Village," A said, looking down at them and smiling.

"Um, thank you," Groog answered, feeling unsettled by having to stare up at the man. He wanted to stand, but being unfamiliar with local customs, he didn't want to appear rude.

"You changed your name when you became leader?" Dag asked.

"Yes. Now, what's this business about an approaching army?"

"Right." Groog regained his wits. "They're a group of people called WeFolk. They are brutal and they are strong. We believe they're coming here to lay siege to your village."

"The Village," corrected A.

"Lay siege to your The Village," Groog said.

"Our wall is very sturdy and very high. And our ranks number nearly one hundred."

"This is all true, and you might well repel their invasion. But I saw them murder my friend for no reason at all and felt it my duty to warn you."

A thought about this for a moment and nodded. “Thank you.” Then he looked back at his pictures of words. Now that A had heard their warning, the meeting was clearly over.

“There is one other thing,” Groog said.

“Yes?”

“Fire.”

“Fire?” A looked up.

“A sign outside said something about a ‘Fire Shop’ coming soon. We would like some, please.”

“Ah.”

And that was all A said. The group was finding his manner of speech, with frequent and long breaks, unnerving. This was intentional on A’s part. It was his way of keeping opponents off balance, a skill he had practiced for many hours. The trick turned out to be instrumental in ascending to the leadership of The Village.

“So,” Groog said, again being the first to break the silence, “may we have some fire?”

“How will you pay for it?”

“Pay?”

“Yes, do you have any money?” Groog looked at Oog, Dag, and Clint, all of whom shrugged. “Hmmmm,” A said. “Where do you come from?”

“Home,” Oog answered without thinking.

“And in this ‘The Home,’ A began.

“Not The Home, just Home.”

“I see. And in this Home, how do you trade things? If...” He motioned toward Dag.

“Dag,” Oog said, taking her hand.

“If Dag has something you want, how do you treat with her to get it? Do you just take it from her, or do you trade?"

"I ask her for it."

"But you must return something of value."

Oog thought about this and looked at Groog. His old mentor scrunched up his mouth and shrugged his shoulders.

"I show her my appreciation?" Oog half-asked, half-stated, turning back to A.

A raised one eyebrow, tilted his head, and turned to address Dag. "And you would give this valued treasure to..."

"Oog," Dag said, and squeezed his hand tighter.

"And you would give this valued treasure to Oog?"

"It depends."

"Ah," A said, and again paused.

"It depends," Dag continued "on whether or not I'm using it. If I am, Oog can wait. If I'm not, I will give it to him."

"And what if he doesn't give it back?"

"Why would I do that?" Oog asked.

"I don't know, maybe you simply want it. Maybe you believe you need it more than Dag."

"Why can't we just share it?" Dag asked.

"Because that is not in our nature."

"It's in my nature," Groog said. Oog and Dag muttered their agreement. Only Clint was silent. A turned to him.

"And you? You would not give it back?"

"No, I would," he answered heavily, "But I have seen those who would not."

"The WeFolk?" Groog asked.

Clint nodded. "They claim everything is owned by everybody, so no one can have anything."

A strong gust of wind blew outside, kicking dust through the window and making the building shudder and groan.

"Is this what you do here in this The Village? You take things and don't give them back?" Oog asked.

"No, my dear man, no. We pay for things. With money."

"What is money?" Groog asked.

"Money represents value." A set aside the thin piece of wood with the words and became animated for this first time. "Let's say I have a sharpened stick. You have the pelts of two Fat Squirrels, and Dag has some deliciously ripe berries."

"Yes," Groog said, listening, as they all were, in rapt attention.

"How do you decide who has the best thing? The thing worth the most?"

"It's the sharpened stick," Clint offered.

"No, it's the berries," Oog interjected.

"The stick can be used for protection, or to hunt food."

"The berries are food."

"Exactly!" A clapped his hands together.

"Exactly what?" Dag asked.

"You need another measure, something outside and impartial, to determine value. That's what money is. We have developed a system to say that a sharpened stick, a Fat Squirrel pelt, and delicious berries all have value related to one another, but also independent of one another."

Oog, Dag, and Clint looked bewildered. Groog nodded. "I think I understand," he said. "You use this mon-ey," he sounded out the word carefully, looking up to make sure he had it right. A smiled and nodded for Groog to go on. "You use this money to trade for things. I might give you one money for a Fat Squirrel pelt, but five money for a sharpened stick. Is that right?"

"Yes!" A clapped his hands together again. "That is exactly right! Very good, Groog, very good. It usually takes outsiders a long time to grasp this concept."

"And we need money to pay for the fire?"

"Right again!" A answered with enthusiasm.

Groog, finding confidence in his ability to follow A's explanation, rose to his knees. "Wonderful. May we have some money, please? We would like to pay for the fire now."

50.

The march of the WeFolk army was relentless. They trudged on, moving in unison, mostly silent, entirely glum.

No Name had continued his stilted conversation with Buh-ohb, learning as many words as he could force his brain to remember. And there were many.

Once or twice he and Buh-ohb had strayed into the confusing realm of intangible things—how do you convey a word for a concept like worry or curiosity?—before returning to the more approachable catalog of identifiable nouns. Bird, tree, worm, acorn, sky, ground, sun, and on and on. No Name practiced each new word he learned.

During a break, as the WeFolk relieved themselves and foraged for food, No Name tried to pantomime the thing he coveted most, wanting desperately to learn its name. He pretended to come close to something warm and bright, and then backed away, doing his best to feign cold and dark.

"The sun?" Buh-ohb asked.

"No. No the sun," No Name said with the halting accent of someone just learning a language. He then pointed to the ground and made the same motions. Buh-ohb made a great show of thinking about No Name's movements before suddenly exclaiming, "Ah! Fire. You mean fire."

No Name had heard the word before, at the camp he had attacked, and knew it must be correct. He was so excited he started jumping up and down, hooting and hollering, and loudly repeating the word. "Fi-er! Fi-er!"

Other WeFolk heard this and panicked.

"Where? Where?"

"No!" Bob shouted, trying to calm down the members of his group. "No fire!"

"Yes, fire!" No Name shouted back, thinking Buh-ohb was talking to him.

The confusion only made the WeFolk panic more. "Where's the fire?" "Are we on fire?" "By we, do you mean we are on fire, or we are on fire?" "Does it matter which of us is on fire?" People started running to and fro in a panic. Only the three leaders—Tall Man, Short Man, and the Woman—seemed to remain calm.

"Where's the fire!?" someone shouted again.

"There is no fire!" Bob yelled.

"Yes, fire!" No Name responded with glee.

"Will you please stop that?" Bob shouted. "I told you, there is no fire!"

At the use of the words "you" and "I," everyone in the camp froze. Someone muttered, "Ooooh."

"I'm sorry," Bob said, fear in his voice. "I mean, er, uh, we mean, we're sorry."

Tall Man came over to Bob. "We are not amused." All eyes were trained on Bob and the unfolding scene.

"What shall we do with us?" the Woman asked, shaking her head. "This is not our first offense. Nor our second." Her tone was sharp.

"Let's stone us!" someone shouted. "We haven't had a good stoning in ages."

"No," an older, grizzled voice jumped in, "stoning is too good for us. We deserve something far worse."

"Such as?"

"We don't know, bonk us on the head?"

"What do you think happens in a stoning?" These last words were spoken by a young man who realized his own mistake as soon as it was out of his mouth. "What do we think happens in a stoning," he corrected.

"Maybe we should bonk us on the head," the fan of stonings said to him.

"Enough," the Woman said, "enough. This will be our final warning," she told Bob. "We will abide by the conventions of our community, or we will suffer the consequences."

"Like a stoning!"

Bob didn't want to be stoned, or suffer any other consequences, whatever they might be. "We understand," he said with great remorse, "and we are sorry."

"Now," Tall Man said, "let us resume our pursuit of the Grooooog and the Ooooog. We must repel our invasion."

There were general noises of agreement as the band of WeFolk started its march once again. And again, Bob and No Name found themselves at the back of the line.

"Buh-ohb," No Name said softly. "We," he tapped his own chest, "sorry."

Bob looked at No Name with surprise and smiled. "That's okay, little fella. We're just learning."

While No Name didn't understand the words, he knew they were said in friendship. For the first time in his life, No Name felt something akin to affection. It was odd and pleasing, and somehow made him feel anxious.

When the army halted its march and No Name looked up, he found himself facing a large, seemingly impenetrable wall.

51.

After the departure of Conifo and Decidua, and with the Formerly-Great-and-Powerful-and-Now-Utterly-Banished Zook, Bilga, and Cagu driven into exile, Krog, quite unexpectedly, found himself the de facto leader of a group of people he hardly knew. It was made all the more difficult by the language barrier between the People Who Liked Trees and the People Who Liked Other People but Didn't Seem to Like Dag.

In addition to Krog, there was one other member of Cagu's small army—Tacitus—who spoke both the Tree Language and the common tongue of the Forest. With Krog and Tacitus translating, there was considerable discussion over the name of the new, melded group.

"We should be the People and Tree Likers!"

"No, that sounds too much like People and Tree Lickers."

"Well, then how about the Sun Lickers?"

"We don't want to be the anything lickers!"

"What about the People Who Like Trees and Also Like Other People?"

"'Most Other People," someone interjected.

"What?"

"I didn't like that Dag woman very much."

"I don't know. The People Who Like Trees and Also Like Most

Other People seems like a bit of a mouthful, doesn't it?"

There were murmurs of agreement.

"What about—?"

It went on like this for quite some time before Krog stepped in and chose the new name: The People Who Like Each Other and Trees.

It was his first act as a leader, and he found having responsibility suited him. He liked the variety of challenges he had to face, thriving on the pressure.

His second decision was to send a scouting party in search of Oog and Dag. Krog's heart was still heavy at the memory of how he and his friends had parted. Add to that the warning of the giant trees about 'strange things being afoot in the Forest,' and Krog had all the motivation he needed.

The scouting party, which included Tacitus the translator, departed the camp the following morning.

NOTES ON MARKETING

More generations after the time of Oog than a person could count—to be honest, most people could count that high; they were just lazy and inexplicably distrusted math—a man named Gary Dahl became a multimillionaire by having what is widely regarded as the dumbest idea in recorded history.

One night in a bar, Dahl listened to his friends complain about the care and feeding of their pet dogs and cats. "Wouldn't it be easier," Dahl said, "if your pets were rocks?"

"Sure, Gary, sure," one of them is purported to have remarked. "Maybe it's time we called you a cab."

They did, and Gary stumbled into his home where he sat down and wrote a document called "The Care and Training of Your Pet Rock." Liking what he created, Dahl decided to take the idea and run with it.

"Sure, Gary, sure," his friends said. "A pet rock. An idea that just can't miss." Then they would roll their eyes.

But Gary would not be deterred. He created a square box in which he put straw, and on top of which he laid a smooth, round stone. He added his care and training manual, and voila, a Pet Rock.

Gary's friends stopped rolling their eyes when Gary's money started rolling in. He sold one million pet rocks for the price of four dollars each.

In Oog's time, a thinker named Crag kept a rock as a pet. He took the rock everywhere he went, spoke to it quietly when he thought others were out of earshot, and turned his back when the rock, which he had coincidentally named Gary, needed to relieve itself.

Crag was a member of the WeFolk tribe and was banished when he was found trying to derive carnal pleasure from and with the rock. (Gary the Rock stayed with the WeFolk for a year after his master was exiled, eventually leaving to go in search of psychotherapy. Sadly, he was millennia too early, as the science hadn't yet been invented.)

The story of the two Garys and the Pet Rocks just goes to show that one person's marketing is another person's crazy.

52.

A gritted his teeth and ran his fingers through his hair. "Let me try this again. I cannot just give you money. You have to earn it."

"But why?" Oog asked for the third time. "We'll just give the money back when we're done."

"You won't have it when you're done."

"Why?"

A sighed and sat forward on the edge of his chair. "Listen. You want fire, yes?"

"Yes."

"And you need money to buy fire."

"Well, we don't think so. But that's what you keep saying and this is your The Village."

"And you don't have any money."

"No, we don't," said Dag. "We never heard of the stuff before today."

"If I give you money to buy fire, how will I get it back?"

"The person who gives us the fire—"

"Sells you the fire."

"The person who sells us the fire, will give it back to you."

"No," A answered, his voice thick with exasperation, "they won't. They will keep it. Then you'll have fire, the person who sold you the fire will have the money, and I will have nothing. What's in it for me?"

"You will have helped us."

"But why would I want to?" A's voice went up in volume.

"Because," offered Groog, "it's what thinking people do."

"It's what foolish people do. Here, in The Village, you must have a way to pay for money you borrow, and that is done through trade or work to pay off your debt."

"Debt?"

"A word to represent the money you owe."

"What happens if someone takes something, like fire, and they can't pay?" Dag asked.

"They are put to work."

Everyone paused and looked at one another. Then Dag wrinkled her brow, as if she was starting to understand. "Put to work?"

"Yes. Your work is given a certain value. You work until the value of the labor given is equal to what you owe."

"I see." Dag said.

"And, of course," A added, "you will need a place to sleep and food to eat while you're working off your debt. The cost of these things will be added to what you owe."

"Can we see where you keep your fire?" Oog asked.

A paused and some of the color drained from his face. "Well..." he began, and his voice trailed off.

"Yes?" said Oog.

"Well, we don't actually have any fire, per se."

"I'm sorry?" Dag asked with a mixture of confusion and annoyance.

"Well, we had it. But there was an accident with a barrel of water and a lever."

"What's a barrel?" asked Oog.

"What's a lever?" asked Clint.

"Can't you make more?" asked Dag.

"Not as such, or not yet, anyway. Our research and development team is getting close, though. We expect to have it back any day now. If you had some money now, you could put a down paym—"

At that moment, Felipe burst through the door. "A, they're here," he said through heaving breaths.

"Who's here?"

"The invading army."

53.

What business do you have here?" A was standing on the platform inside the wall, the spot usually occupied by Felipe, and was calling down to the invaders, who were still safely outside The Village.

Down below A, on the inside of the gate, were Oog, Dag, Groog, and Clint. The guard who had stood watch outside the door to A's house had been joined by six more and had escorted them here. Each of the guards carried a sharpened stick. Oog looked at them now and realized they, too, were an army.

There is an army on each side of this wall, he thought, and I am trapped between them. This can't be good.

"We demand the release of the Grooooog and the Oooooog," a voice called in answer to A's question.

"So we can stone them!" added another voice, farther away.

"Would we please shut up about stoning?" the first voice answered.

"On what do you base this demand?" A asked.

"We are not you, we are we, and the fugitives harbored behind these walls ate the people's food and drank the people's water without permission."

A looked down at his guests. "You told me you came here to warn us of an invading army. You neglected to mention you were escaped prisoners from that same army."

"We did and we are not," protested Groog. "We don't know why they pursue us. Perhaps it is a ruse to get you to open your gate." This was not entirely true, but Groog was learning quickly that truth was both malleable and, at times, in the eye of the beholder.

No, wait, that isn't right, he thought. *Truth is still truth. What has changed are the people observing it. Truth is absolute. People are not.* He looked at Oog, longing to share this observation with him. *I must remember this for later,* he thought.

"Perhaps," A said to Groog, "I don't know what to believe." His face was stern. He turned his attention back to the other side of the wall.

"I see," A said in response. "They took your property without compensating you."

"No. We do not believe in compensation. Or property. All the people share all the property. As such, no people may have it."

"Wait," someone else said from the other side of the wall. "That doesn't sound quite right. Shouldn't it be that everyone can have it?"

"Only when we all say it is allowed," the first voice answered.

"Now, when we say we, do we mean—?"

"With whom am I speaking?" A interrupted.

"We are the WeFolk."

A leaned forward and squinted. "You don't look especially small."

"We told us it was bad name," came a new voice from over the wall. There were murmurs of agreement.

"Quiet!" the first voice said. "And with whom are we speaking?"

"I am A."

There was a long pause before a different voice on the other side of the wall answered with, “A what?”

“Just A.”

“It can’t be *just* A. It has to be ‘a’ something. A pointed stick, a Fat Squirrel.”

“I bet that happens a lot,” Dag whispered to Oog. He nodded.

“My name is A, just A. And we cannot give you the fugitives without getting something in return.”

“We are not fugitives!” Groog shouted.

“Was that one of them?” asked the main speaker for the WeFolk. “Was that the Grooooog or the Oooooog?”

A ignored both Groog and the question from the other side of the fence. “Again, what will you give us in return?”

There was a long pause as a low thrum of murmuring came from the WeFolk. Oog couldn’t make out any of what was being spoken, but his power of thought told him the WeFolk were debating what to do. The conversation seemed to go on for a long time.

“Listen,” A said. “Just pull the rope to ring the bell when you’ve got it figured out.” He started to climb down from the platform.

“Wait!” came a voice. “We will give you the one formerly known as Bob.”

“What?” cried another voice. Oog supposed that would be Bob.

“And what value does Bob have?” A asked.

“What value,” the voice shot back, “do the Groooog and the Oooog have?”

A paused and considered this. “I will release one of the fugitives in exchange for Bob.”

The response came without hesitation. “We agree.”

There was a tumult of shouts on both sides of the wall, with Oog,

Groog, Dag, and Bob protesting all at once. Others added their voices to the fray, too.

"Quiet!" A's tone of voice was meant to command attention and it worked. Everyone fell silent. He turned his gaze to two of his guards. "Open the gate."

54.

No Name watched as an old man surrounded by four young men, the latter carrying pointed sticks, emerged from an opening in the strange wooden mountain. What had Buh-ohb called it? A wall? And the opening a gate? He recognized the old man immediately as one of the two fire tenders from the camp of the old people. Behind him, still standing inside the wall, was the younger fire tender. No Name understood very few of the gibberish words that had been shouted between the two armies, though he sensed these proceedings were important.

So focused was No Name on the two fire tenders, he didn't at first notice several of the WeFolk pushing and shoving Buh-ohb toward the gate. Buh-ohb protested for a moment before his shoulders and chin drooped, and he marched forward with resignation.

They must be trading people, No Name thought. *But why?*

The old fire tender stopped at the edge of the barrier, looking back with longing. One of the guards made his pointed stick horizontal with the ground and used the butt end of it to shove the old man forward. He stumbled a step before righting himself and walked toward the WeFolk with his head held high and his shoulders back.

"Groooooooog," Tall Man said, drawing the name out and smiling, like they were old acquaintances.

"It's just Groog."

"That's not what the other one said," Tall Man answered.

"Because you were torturing him at the time."

Without warning, Tall Man swung his foot, sweeping out both of Groog's legs and causing him to fall backwards.

While everyone else remained frozen, the younger fire tender instinctively started forward, but a hand stopped him. It was the female at his side.

"The Rock of Justice," Tall Man bellowed. He held out his hand without taking his eyes from Groog. Short Man carefully unfolded an animal skin and removed a large rock, one end of which had been sharpened to a point.

No Name had seen this rock once before; Tall Man had used it to kill the man the WeFolk had tortured. No Name understood immediately that Tall Man meant to use it again now. If that was true, then would the people behind the wall use their own special rock to kill Buh-ohb, his first and only friend? Is this what large groups of thinkers did? Trade people and kill them?

"Buh-ohb," No Name whimpered.

For neither the first nor the last time, No Name cursed all this thinking.

Tall Man turned the rock on its blunt end and raised it high over Groog's head. Then, he turned to address A and everyone else assembled. "Let this be a lesson," he said, "to any who would stand against we the people!"

55.

Groog braced himself for the end.

The sun, now low in the sky, caught a small piece of quartz embedded in the rock Tall Man was brandishing, throwing a rainbow prism at Groog's eye. In it, he saw his life:

The first time he had a conscious thought, as a teenager, wondering why trees didn't fall over.

The day he met Mother and the warm touch of her hand on his face.

The night of the storm in which he learned to tame fire.

The day Oog ran into the camp like a raving lunatic.

Oog. He knew his friend—no, more than his friend, his family—he knew Oog, his family, was back there somewhere. Groog only hoped Oog would do nothing foolish.

"Let this be a lesson," Tall Man said to everyone listening, "to any who would stand against we the people!" He turned his attention back to Groog. "Though, we don't know," he said so only Groog could hear. "Maybe our rock is too good for you. Aren't you, baby?" Groog wasn't sure, but he thought Tall Man might have been talking to the rock. His suspicion deepened when Tall Man nuzzled the killing rock against his cheek and lightly kissed its smooth surface.

Groog looked to the other WeFolk, but none seemed to see—or maybe it was that they refused to acknowledge—what was happening. Even Short Man and the Woman were averting their eyes.

"You're mad," Groog said.

"Not mad, baby. Just crazy."

Then, without warning, Tall Man swung his foot hard into Groog's head, and laughed. Groog, dazed and hurt, was still conscious enough to hear the laugh. *One man's laughter is another's doom,* he thought. *Oh, that's a good one. I only hope I live long enough to tell Oog.*

56.

Let this be a lesson," Tall Man said, "to any who would stand against we the people!"

It took Oog a minute to understand the meaning of the words. Tall Man was going to kill Groog, then and there.

Oog couldn't wait any longer. He shook off Dag's arm and took off through the gate, running as fast as he could. He made a straight line—Groog had once taught Oog the shortest distance between two points was a straight line—toward where Tall Man held the sharpened rock high in the air. Behind him, Dag screamed, "Oog! No!"

Oog didn't break stride. He couldn't.

Halfway there, Oog saw Tall Man change tactics and kick Groog in the head, hard.

"Not nice!" Oog shouted. "Not. Nice!"

Tall Man peered over his shoulder and spotted Oog barreling toward him. Rather than take a defensive posture, Tall Man once again raised the Rock of Justice and turned back to Groog.

Dazed from being kicked in the head, Groog's arm probed the ground around him, his hand finding a fist-sized stone. He wrapped his fingers around an end of it and lifted it just in time to defend the blow of the killing rock.

Tall Man's rock crashed onto and careened off of Groog's stone. Only, Groog realized, it wasn't a stone at all; its underside was coated in an oozing slime. He was holding a Speeder Snail.

Groog used all his strength to hold the small living shield—the only thing between him and certain death—aloft. Tall Man struck a second time, the killing rock making contact with the shell and glancing off again. With each blow, the tiny creature who lived in the shell, whose name was Brian, let out a small yelp of dismay. While no humans could hear the yelp, a passing Speeder Snail, whose name was Graham, heard the distressing call and quickened his pace, leaving poor Brian to fend for himself.

Just as Oog was preparing to knock Tall Man to the ground, the killing rock came down a third time. Tall Man's swing was so hard, the rock striking the calcified shell with so much force, sparks shot up and fell to the ground, forming a halo around Groog's head.

The sight caused Oog to stop short.

Sparks.

Groog had seen it, too.

The two men—father and son in every way that mattered—locked eyes and started laughing.

Sparks.

Fire.

"Fi-er!" someone shouted.

"Fire?" one of the WeFolk answered in a panic. "Where?"

Tall Man, confused at the laughter and at the growing chorus of people shouting fire, paused just long enough for Groog to give one final piece of advice to Oog. "Run," he croaked with what little voice he had left. "Just, run."

Oog was a bubbling stew of conflicting emotions. He was

awestruck, confused, hopeful, helpless, terrified.

The secret of fire, he thought. He knew in an instant what it would mean, how many people would be helped, and how the balance of power in the Forest would be tipped.

Fire. I know how to make fire.

"Run," Groog said again, summoning the strength to say it this time with more urgency.

"I don't think so," Tall Man said. He nodded at the nearest of the WeFolk guards, two of whom regained their wits and sprang into action.

Without stopping to consider the consequences, Oog heeded Groog's advice and sprinted away from The Village. He looked over his shoulder and spied his pursuers, two strong men. Beyond them, Oog saw Tall Man mutter some words to Groog, then bring his rock down a final time, shattering Brian's shell just before it shattered Groog's skull.

"Aaaaaarrrrrrggggghhhhhhhhh!"

The wail of pain that reverberated off the walls of the fence and shook the trees at the edge of the clearing didn't come from Groog, or even from Brian. It came from Oog, his anguish a new and living thing brought into the world. The scream—so loud, so guttural, so ancient—caused the horrifying tableau to step apart from the passage of time: Oog frozen in mid-stride, looking back at his dying friend and mentor, his mind and soul aflame with sorrow and rage; the WeFolk guards momentarily stunned into immobility; Dag, Clint, and A, jaws agape and bodies unmoving; and Tall Man standing over the bleeding and dying body of Groog.

It wasn't until Dag cried Oog's name again—"Oog!"—and the gate in the wall started to close, that time lurched forward once more. Oog resumed his run; the WeFolk resumed their pursuit.

Oog was fast and nimble. He had, after all, spent a disproportionate amount of his thinking life running. But the WeFolk men were older, larger, and better conditioned, and slowly they were gaining ground.

Oog made it to the trees. He hoped he could lose his hunters by being clever, by using a combination of agility and guile. He darted this way and that, changed directions suddenly, and ran through a thicket of bushes.

But still, they closed the gap.

He knew if he could not outrun them, he would die. The guards would bring him back to the WeFolk, and he, Oog, would meet the same fate as Groog.

Oog pivoted around a large eucalyptus tree and was nearly startled out of his skin as he ran into four men, knocking one to the ground. The men carried pointed sticks and wooden shields. Oog collected himself and caught his breath.

The men seemed as startled as Oog.

"Oog?" said one.

Oog looked closer at the man. He knew him. But how?

"Nos sunt vultus pro vobis," the young man said. "Esne bene?"

A Person of the Tree! Had they pursued Oog all this way?

"If you don't understand his gibberish," one of the other men said, "I can translate. He says we've been looking for you—"

Just at that moment, the two WeFolk guards rounded the eucalyptus. They, too, stopped dead in their tracks on seeing the unexpected assemblage of people. They took in the scene, looked at one another, and started running again. Oog braced himself for a bonk on the head, or to be tackled, or to at least get a stern talking to, but the guards blew past him and just kept on going.

Oog was so confused that he called after them. “Wait? Where are you going?”

“Escaping,” one called back over his shoulder. “If you’re smart, you’ll do the same. Those fuckers are crazy!” And the two guards kept on running.

“What’s going on?” asked the man, the one who wasn’t speaking the language of the People of the Tree.

Oog looked at the man and his companions with a total lack of understanding as to who they were and why they were there. Then he shook his head. *Fire,* he thought. *Fire.*

“I wish I knew,” said Oog, and he was off and running again, too.

“Wait!” the man called, but Oog didn’t stop.

NOTES ON FRIENDSHIP

A study by the University of Olympus Mons on Mars, in the year 2637, conclusively identified the three most complicated systems of interconnectivity in the universe.

Third was quantum mechanics. While the theory of quantum mechanics had long been verified by direct experimentation, it still made little sense to anyone who tried to understand it. Most people thought the cat in the box had to be dead or alive, whether or not someone looked at it. After all, a tree that fell in the forest, contrary to what some physicists might have you believe, made a sound no matter what.

Second on the list was any country's or planet's postal system. Relying on the principles of quantum mechanics, the authors showed that the more a person anticipates the delivery of a package, the longer it takes to arrive. A corollary to this was the theory of lost luggage, which stated that the greater the need for something in your roller bag, the less likely it was to arrive on time, or at its intended destination, and certainly not both simultaneously.

It was, however, the most complicated system of interconnectivity that proved to be the most controversial. According to the study, the system of friendship that exists between any two people was orders of magnitude more complicated than any system identified anywhere or at anytime in the known universe. The research—which included the invention of a new form of math called amitymatics—showed an increasing correlation between platonic intimacy and friendly rivalry. In other words, while to know someone is to love them, it is also true that familiarity does, in fact, breed contempt.

After receiving their Nobel Prize, the two lead authors, lifelong friends, would not speak to one another for twenty years. When they finally reunited, it was with great skepticism and mistrust.

57.

No Name watched in fascination as the young fire tender sprinted through the gate, running at full speed toward the Tall Man and the old fire tender. The young female screamed a word, and a scene of chaos unfolded around them.

In the commotion, No Name saw opportunity.

"Buh-ohb!" he called. "Buh-ohb! Friend!"

Bob heard the strange little man calling his name. With everyone distracted by Oog's mad dash, Bob bolted back through the gate and toward No Name. Just as he arrived, Tall Man brought his rock down toward the old fire tender with such force, smashing it against a rock his captive held out in defense, that he created a shower of sparks. Both Bob and No Name saw it.

"Fi-er!" No Name shouted.

"Fire? Where?" The confusion reached a fever pitch.

Before either Bob or No Name knew what was happening, the young fire tender had taken flight. An instant later, Tall Man brought his rock down a final time, splitting the old fire tender's defensive stone, and murdering the man in cold blood and in plain sight.

(None of the humans taking part in this drama, save Groog, were aware of the fate of Brian the Speeder Snail. Graham the Speeder Snail, who had moments earlier fled the scene, would go on to pen a long lament called “The Strange Heroic Journey of Brian,” that is sung to snail children to this day. It’s a four-part dirge told mostly through the secretion of oozing slime.)

Not pausing to think—or rather, thinking very, very fast—No Name grabbed Bob’s arm and spoke one of the few verbs he had managed to learn. “Come.”

And they were off and running.

58.

After leaving the four strangers in the woods, Oog altered his course to follow the curve of The Village wall, heading back in the direction from which he'd come. He stayed under the cover of trees but kept the wall in sight. A torrent of thoughts was coursing through his mind:

Why did those WeFolk guards say they were 'escaping?'

What are People of the Tree doing in this part of the Forest? Have they come for me?

Are Dag and Clint now prisoners of The Village People?

Is there going to be war between the WeFolk and The Village People?

Will I be able to make fire?

One more thought kept trying to brute force its way into Oog's consciousness, but he was steadfast in his refusal to allow it in: Groog. He was not ready to mourn his friend or to try to make sense of not only Groog's death, but death in general. He needed to complete his mission first.

Oog came to the trail he and his friends had followed to find The Village, turned right, and was quickly back at the place where the trail joined another, forming, if traveling in the other direction, a fork. He continued on until he came to the tree where he and Groog had been reunited. Again, images of Groog tried to take hold of Oog's thinking, but Oog willed them away. At least for now.

The marks Oog had left on the trees were still visible, pointing him in the direction he needed to travel.

Moving at a run, he covered what he believed was the largest amount of ground, in the shortest amount of time, in the history of human beings.

Point in fact, it was the third most ground covered at record speed.

The second most was by a non-thinker who had unwittingly sat on a colony of fire ants. The ants had found their way into the non-thinker's more delicate spots, making the non-thinker jump and run. His fight or flight response was all flight, only you can't outrun something stuck up your bum.

The most ground covered at record speed was by a lone thinking woman named Ryley. She simply liked to run far and fast, and was very, very good at it.

It was nightfall as Oog descended beneath the canopy of trees, found the stream, and made his way back into the heart of Town.

Most of the Townsfolk were gathered around the fire telling stories and were startled and alarmed when Oog came to a stop and collapsed in front of them. He sank to his knees gulping for air and splayed his hands on the dusty earth.

Trish, Sica, and Em gathered around Oog and helped him sip water. It was several minutes before he could move or even talk. When he caught his breath, they guided him to a log, put an animal skin around his shoulders, and waited.

At long last, Oog regained enough composure to tell his story. He spared no detail, sharing all that had transpired since he had left this same fire a mere two days before. It felt like a lifetime.

When he got to the murder of Groog, he couldn't stop from

breaking down a little—water flowed from his eyes—but he wouldn't let go completely. Sica tried to wrap him in an embrace, but Oog squirmed away.

"Fire," he finally said. "We need to make fire."

59.

After Bilga, Cagu, and Zook were banished by the strange talking trees—Bilga was still scratching his head over that one—they entered the wilds of the Forest. Bilga looked at his companions and shook his head.

"All right, boys, where to?"

"Quid?" Cagu asked.

Bilga didn't understand the word but he grokked the meaning. "We're going to need to find a way to communicate," he answered. "Do you understand any of our words?" he asked, speaking very slowly.

"Little," Cagu replied, making a small gesture with his thumb and forefinger.

Zook perked up at this. "Cool, man, cool. Do you understand that I really like you?" he said to Cagu and started walking toward him. Cagu put up a hand to stop him and looked at Bilga.

"Id-dee-it?"

Bilga let out of sharp laugh. "Yes, idiot. C'mon. Let's keep moving. We need to find water before nightfall."

They moved deeper into the Forest, Zook trying to like a variety of small game, shrubs, and rocks, all with no success, and Cagu studying each tree they passed with increasing fear and paranoia, wondering which ones would come to life and castigate him. As the Forest was stocked with an unending supply of trees, Cagu devolved into a kind of manic state.

Bilga's mood soured as the day wore on, wondering why he had left. "My idiot son," he muttered to himself, "that's why."

"Quid?" Cagu asked, his voice quaking.

Bilga looked squarely at Cagu, remembering this man was responsible for the death of the gate keeper at his village. "There is really no way this ends well, is—"

"Freeze! We're under arrest!"

Two men with red smeared on their faces and carrying pointed sticks leapt out from behind a tree, making Bilga, Cagu, and Zook jump back.

"What the hell!?" Bilga shouted. "You scared the crap out of me!"

Both of the WeFolk guards peered around Bilga's backside to see if they had scared the actual crap out of him.

They had not.

"We're under arrest," one of the guards tried again.

"You're under arrest and you want us to help you?" Bilga asked, confused.

"No," the guard answered, "we," he used his hand to indicate Bilga and his two compatriots, "are under arrest."

"We?" Bilga asked, touching his own chest.

"Yes!" The guard seemed relieved Bilga understood his meaning.

"On whose authority do you arrest us?" Bilga asked.

"On the authority of the WeFolk. We seek those with knowledge of the Ooooog, and we demand—"

"WeFolk? You don't look small."

"Oog?" Cagu asked, his ears perked up.

No one noticed that Zook had crept up to the second guard from the side. He dabbed his forearm with a bit of dried green paint peeled from his own skin.

"Hey!" the guard exclaimed, wheeling on him.

"It's okay," Zook said, "I really like you."

"Iste homo stultus est."

"Huh?" the guard asked, not understanding the strange words.

Bilga shook his head in disgust. "You know what?" he said, putting his hands in the air. "Forget it. My name is Bilga, and this is Zook, and this is Cagu. And we are guilty of...well, whatever it was you said we were guilty of. Now, arrest us. Please."

60.

Krog's men had been so startled by Oog suddenly appearing on the other side of a eucalyptus tree, and by the pursuing WeFolk guards and their strange behavior, they never had a chance to explain to Oog why they were there.

By the time the quartet regained its collective wits, Oog had already taken flight. They tried to follow, but he was too fast.

When the party returned home, Tacitus reported back to Krog.

"Oog was being chased?" Krog asked.

"Yes."

"But his pursuers kept running, claiming they were escaping?"

"Yes.

"And you don't know from what?"

"No."

"And there was an encampment with a wall even bigger than ours?"

"Yes, much bigger."

"And you say Oog was alone?"

"He was."

None of this made sense.

Where was Dag? And what was this wall? And who was chasing Oog and what were they "escaping" from?

"Lead me to the spot where you last saw him," Krog said, deciding he needed more information before he could plan a course of action.

He assembled a small band of twenty people, including the four guards from the scouting party, and they marched toward The Village, only two hours away. They had come down the main road and were facing the entry gate. The group moved to the edge of the clearing, staying hidden in the woods, observing.

A large cadre of people with red smeared on their faces was already standing outside the wall. One of the red-faced people was talking with a clean-faced person who was looking down from the other side of the wall. Krog could hear their voices but wasn't close enough to make out their words.

"Listen," Krog whispered to his troops, "I'm going out there to see what this is all about. Stay hidden unless I call for you." He then repeated the words in the language of the People of the Tree. In his mind, he had started to call it Tree Language and yearned for the day when everyone under his charge spoke a common tongue. For now, he would have to make do.

Krog's comrades nodded and he stepped into the clearing, only thirty paces from the WeFolk army. He was surprised to see Bilga, Cagu, and the Formerly-Great-and-Powerful-and-Now-Utterly-Banished Zook kneeling between the red-faced people and the wall. Just then, a gate in the wall started to open.

Short Man had been jumpy during the entire escapade at the gate of The Village. The sheer size of the wall, combined with the refusal of The Village's leader—this strange man with the strange name of "A"—to be cowed by Tall Man, led Short Man to believe they were in over their heads. He was twitchy, looking constantly over his shoulder.

So, he looked over his shoulder.

“Oi!” he shouted at Krog. “Who are we?”

Everyone’s attention turned.

Tall Man looked from Krog to A. “A trap?”

A looked from Krog to Tall Man. “Reinforcements?”

“I am a friend of Oog and Dag,” Krog announced, “and I wish to know what is happening here. I demand to see my friends.”

There was a pause filled with the swarming of gnats rising from the grass; a pause baked by the heat of the sun sinking lower in the sky; a pause that hung like a noose around the absolute calm of the windless afternoon.

In other words, it was a really long pause.

A voice from just inside the open gate exploded across the clearing. Krog knew the voice at once.

Dag.

“RUN!” she screamed.

That’s when all hell broke loose.

61.

After the murder of Groog and the flight of Oog, A had ordered the gate closed and Dag and Clint taken to the "Holding House." Dag hardly noticed the rough, meaty hands grabbing her shoulders and shoving her away from the fence line. "Oog," she half-muttered, half-cried.

She and Clint were led to a small, unremarkable building with only one door. They were shoved inside, the door slamming shut behind them. Unlike A's house, the Holding House had no chairs or animal skins or even wood floors. It was a square room with a packed dirt floor and no windows. Tiny slivers of light crept through seams in the wooden walls, but not enough to overcome the sweltering darkness. Dag collapsed to the ground, crawled to a corner, and cried. She heard Clint beating his fists on the walls and shouting to be let out, but it sounded far away, as if it was from a different part of the Forest. After a time, Dag cried herself into a kind of unconsciousness that could only charitably be called sleep.

She dreamed of home and of her parents. Only, in the dream, her mother was Oog and her father was Groog. They were sleeping in a small, hot room, and she could not wake them. She knew she needed to wake them, to tell them to run. But run from what? It didn't matter. She shook them, but they didn't stir. She tried to scream at them, but she had no voice. She kicked them. She beat her fists on their chests. She—

The thunk of the Holding House door flying open, combined with the light flooding into the room, dragged Dag unceremoniously back to full wakefulness.

"Come on," said a figure in the doorway. She recognized the voice as Felipe, gatekeeper of The Village.

"Finally," Clint said, and strode out of the house. Dag dragged herself up and followed. She was surprised to see the sun so much lower in the sky. She must have slept for hours.

Dag and Clint were met by six The Village People guards who immediately surrounded them.

"What's going on? Where are you taking us?" Clint was midway on the continuum between determined and hysterical. Neither Felipe nor the guards answered.

When they reached the gate, A was standing on the platform. He turned his attention away from whatever was happening on the other side of the wall and addressed Dag and Clint.

"I'm sorry," he called down to them.

"Sorry for what?" Clint called back. "Sorry for being such a jerk?"

"I'm not so sure that kind of talk will help you," Felipe offered.

"Will it hurt us?"

"I suppose not."

"Right, then A is a jerk, a real patch of moss."

With a loud creak and groan, the pane of wood that formed the entrance gate of the wall started to rise.

"Are we being freed?" Dag asked.

"I don't think so." Clint's answer was more an exhale than a sentence.

As the gate rose, the WeFolk army came into view. They formed a semicircle around three men, all on their knees, all with their hands bound, and all sporting bruises and looking much worse for the wear. Dag recognized one of them right away, the Formerly-Great-and-Powerful-and-Now-Utterly-Banished Zook. He was the man who had dabbed her with red paint.

"What is this?" Dag asked Felipe. Then asked the question again, calling up to A. "What is this?"

"Prisoner exchange."

"Oh, shit." Clint turned to run, but two of The Village People guards blocked his escape. They grabbed him by the arms.

At that exact moment, one of the WeFolk troops called out, "Oi, who are we?" Everyone's attention moved past the Tall Man at the head of the army to a man who had stepped out of the woods. He was bathed in sunlight.

"I am a friend of Oog and Dag," the man yelled.

Oh no, Dag thought, Krog. What's he doing? He's going to get himself killed.

"And I wish to know what is happening here. I demand to see my friends."

Tall Man looked to A. "A trap?"

A shook his head no. "Reinforcements?" he asked.

Tall Man shook his head. He then raised an arm toward Krog and spoke two simple words. They were too soft for Krog to hear, but not Dag. "Get us," he said.

"Now when you say us—" one of the WeFolk guards started.

"RUN!" Dag's bellow, it would be said years later, could be heard from one end of the Forest to the other.

But instead of running, Krog raised his own arm, and then wordlessly brought it down. To Dag's and everyone else's surprise, nearly two dozen men and women, armed with pointed sticks and shields, stepped out of the Forest and fanned out, forming a line on either side of Krog.

Tall Man looked from Krog to his prisoners. "Right," he said, addressing A. "The enemy of our enemy is our friend. Wouldn't we agree?"

All it took was a simple nod from A for the WeFolk to spring into action. Dag was nearly bowled over as Tall Man ushered his troops and prisoners inside the wall, just as A was ordering his men to close the gate.

There was a moment of eerie silence when the gate made a final thud, sealing The Village People, WeFolk, Dag, and Clint inside the gate, and Krog and his People Who Like Each Other and Trees outside.

Everyone inside the gate was momentarily frozen. Dag was about to demand her release when a jagged rock landed at her feet. It was followed by another rock, and then another.

Krog and his army were making it rain stones in The Village. Everyone inside the fence scattered.

62.

The next morning, a team of Town elders sat with Oog as he banged a rock against the shell of an unlucky Speeder Snail he had found nearby.

"Stop! For the love of all that is holy, stop!" the Speeder Snail, whose name was Gus, screamed. As Speeder Snail speech consisted mostly of oozing secretions, Oog would pause to wipe his hand on the dirt but kept banging the rock.

"Does it have to be a Speeder Snail?" one of the elders asked.

Oog thought about that. "I don't know," he said.

The group then gathered a wide variety of stones: large, jagged rocks; flat, smooth shale; fist-sized granite riddled with quartz; and many more. Oog tried them all.

After an hour, he could recreate the sparks coming off almost any of the stones on command, but the sparks never turned to fire. (Oog, to Gus's great delight, had put the Speeder Snail aside in favor of the rocks. Gus darted away, seeking water to tend his wounds.) And it wasn't just Oog. A group of Town elders were also busy banging rocks; they too were creating sparks, but also with no resulting flame.

Oog knew, he just knew, this was the path to creating fire. Why wasn't it working?

"I am at a loss," Oog said.

"We need to be methodical," replied Aden, the eldest of those in this impromptu group of would-be fire starters. Aden's hair was thin and gray, his skin folded over itself, especially around his neck and hands, but his eyes were keen and alert. Something about him reminded Oog of Groog.

"What is 'meth-od-i-cal?'"

"We need a method, a way, a manner of approaching the problem. We need to try different things, and then to remember what we tried, and what the results were. This will help us narrow down what shows promise and what does not. We will discard ideas that don't work and refine those that do."

"Right," said Oog. "How do we start?"

"Well, let's say out loud everything we know."

"Banging two rocks makes sparks," offered Oog.

"Wood burns," observed Aden.

"Fire hurts," said another.

"Spears of death from the sky make fire."

"Fire is bright and warm."

"It dances. Fire dances."

"Fire makes more fire."

They went on like this until they had exhausted all of their observations.

"Right," said Aden, "so which pieces of information seem most useful for our task?"

"And our task is?" asked one of the Town elders, a woman named Melia. She was nearly as old as Aden and had a propensity for forgetting things.

"To make fire."

"But we have fire."

"Yes, but if we can make fire, it will help many, many people in all parts of the Forest."

"Oh, yes, I see that now."

Oog's mind wandered as Aden explained things to Melia. Patience was a hallmark of the Townsfolk. They truly cared for and loved one another, even if one of them wasn't thinking clearly. It reminded Oog of Dag. She was patient with him. Oog and Dag's plan had been to return to this place and live with these people. He hoped that could still come to pass. He hoped she was safe.

Oog returned to the list of things they knew about fire, identifying three as seeming important:

- Hitting rocks together makes sparks. The sparks seemed, to all of them, to be tiny bits of fire.
- Fire makes more fire. That seemed important. If the sparks were tiny pieces of fire, they should give rise to bigger fire.
- Wood burns.

Wood burns.

"Hey!" Oog said aloud, stopping the conversation. "Wood burns!"

The others understood immediately and, before he knew it, three logs were dropped at Oog's feet. He banged the rocks over the pieces of wood, the sparks showering the logs. A few of the embers smoked, which sent up a cheer from all those assembled, save Melia, who had wandered off.

Oog repeated it over and over, but each time the smoke faded away, the fire failing to take hold. They added dried leaves and smaller twigs, but the result was the same.

The ceaseless motion of banging rocks was making Oog tired, and his hands were developing blisters. What was worse, the absence of wind was causing Oog to drip with sweat.

Wait. Something on the inside of Oog's mind was trying to force its way to the outside. Was it sweating? No. Was it blisters? No. Was it wind? N—"

"Yes!" Oog practically screamed.

"What?" asked Aden.

"Something Groog taught me. Fire eats air."

"But we have plenty of air, do we not?"

"We have no breeze."

"No breeze," muttered Aden and nodded. "Yes, I see."

Oog gritted his teeth through the pain in his hands and banged the rocks again. The sparks rained down on the dried bark of a birch log, and this time Aden bent low to blow on them. The first few attempts blew the sparks off the wood completely.

"Softer," suggested Oog.

They tried again. The embers hit the bark, Aden blew softly, and the amount of smoke increased. Oog kept smashing, Aden kept blowing, and the smoke kept increasing.

And then.

Fire.

Just like that. A tiny flame sprouted on a twig. It didn't last long, but it was there for all to see. The group erupted in shrieks of joy.

"But how do we get it to be more than one small flame?" one of the Elders asked.

Oog looked at Aden and smiled. "We must be methodical."

The group put their heads back together and recounted their observations.

An hour later, they were successfully making fire—sustainable, transferable fire—on command.

They had done it.

NOTES ON WEAPONS

The very first weapon was the human hand. A thinking person used it to slap another thinking person. The reason for the attack is lost to the sea of time, but this dispassionate narrator suspects it had something to do with sex.

From the human hand, weapons progressed in sophistication, but not in purpose or intent. Sticks. Rocks. Sharpened sticks. Sharpened rocks. Bows and arrows. Flaming arrows. Daggers. Swords. Trebuchets. Long bows and long arrows. Catapults. Gunpowder. Rockets. Bombs. Mines. Cannons. Bullets. Hand held guns. Revolving guns. Heavy artillery rockets. Submarines. Naval mines. War ships. Machine guns. Gun silencers. Tanks. Airplanes. Mustard gas. Other chemical weapons. Fully automatic weapons. Atomic fission bombs. Hydrogen fusion bombs. All meant to be used by thinking people to slap other thinking people, mostly for disputes over land, money, and power, or, sometimes, over a dispute about sex.

The first weapon of mass destruction—that is, a weapon that could slap several people at the same time—was a fist-sized piece of granite thrown by a thinker named Heston. The stone bounced off a man's temple, glanced off a woman's shoulder, hit another man in the groin, and landed on a fourth person's foot. Heston was run out of his village by the victims—all of whom survived—and spent the rest of his days being run out of a succession of villages for, unsuccessfully, trying to recreate the incident. Consumed to the point of insanity by his obsession with weapons, he died clutching a rock in his hand, his final words purported to be, "Take your stinking hands off me, you damn, dirty apes," though no one knew why.

Fire, which Oog has just learned to create, was a giver of warmth, cooker of food, and a provider of light. It was also the second weapon of mass destruction ever created. While fire could be used as a singular weapon against an individual, its greater threat was its use against a large number of people. When weaponized, it had the capacity to destroy an entire village.

As Oog was about to discover.

63.

Oog led a group of people from Town back to The Village. They came up out of the canopy of trees, crested the hill, found the path, found the fork in the road, and made it to the wall before the sun was at its apex in the sky.

Traveling with Oog were Sica, Em, Aden, and two of the elders who, like Oog, had proved especially adept at creating fire. There was also a small band of young people who relished the idea of an adventure.

"We must rest here for a moment," Oog said, catching his breath. The others, especially the older members of their band, who were winded as well, collapsed in the grass. Only Aden remained standing.

"This is fascinating." He inspected the wall, touching it with his hands, smelling it, tasting it. Aden once again reminded Oog of Groog, which caused a knot of pain to open in Oog's stomach. Or perhaps it was a cramp from all the running.

"Walls are good for keeping predators out," Sica said.

"They are also good for keeping captives in," Oog answered.

Em, the leader of Town, addressed Oog. "Is the army of which you speak on the other side of this wall?"

"I don't know. We must follow the curve of the wall to the entrance to The Village. When I left, the WeFolk were outside and

The Village People were inside. I don't know what has happened since."

"And our goal here?" Sica asked.

"As I told you, to rescue Dag and Clint."

"And how will you do this?"

"We will use fire."

"You are a keeper of fire. You know the damage it can do if wielded irresponsibly."

"But I will wield it responsibly. I have that power."

Sica was quiet for a long moment, staring at Oog. She shook her head and then looked to her daughter.

"Oog," Em said, laying a gentle hand on his shoulder, "you know we must share the knowledge of how to make fire with others."

"What? No. There are many bad people in the Forest. They will use it for evil."

"Yes, they probably will."

"Then how can you—?"

"If we are the only ones to possess it," Em said, "it will eventually turn us evil."

"No," Oog said. "We are good. You are good. You are wise. Your system of leadership, with a young person guided by a council of elders, is a beautiful thing. Surely neither the leader nor the council would let fire be used for the wrong purpose. And if one did, the other would be there to balance it out."

"Maybe, at first. And maybe for many revolutions of the heavens. But not forever."

"How can you possibly know that?"

"Because power corrupts, and absolute power corrupts absolutely."

There was a loud chattering from the trees as a passing group of Twizzlevarmint guards, agents of the queen, took exception to Em's words. One threw an acorn that landed harmlessly at Oog's feet.

"What do you mean?" he asked.

"If we have fire and no one else does, someday, sometime, we will use it for the wrong reason."

"But I can promise you that both the WeFolk and The Village People will use it for the wrong reason today. It would be folly to share our advantage with our enemies."

"It is your invention and your decision, Oog. But think about this: If we have fire, and the WeFolk have fire, and The Village People have fire, what advantage would either of them have over us? None. They would leave us in peace."

"No," Oog answered. "Their advantage would be a lack of a moral center. They could and would use fire in ways we wouldn't dream of."

"Immorality is not an advantage, it's a handicap."

"It depends on your point of view. The lack of a moral center is seen as a deficit by we who wish to do good. It is seen as a treasure by those who wish to conquer and control."

Oog, Sica, Em, and everyone else sat in silence for a moment thinking about this. Neither side really agreed with the other, but they didn't disagree either. The complicated nature of the debate made Oog long for Groog's advice. He would know right from wrong. He always did. Or maybe he would simply say there was no right or wrong, and you could only do what your heart and mind told you.

But Groog wasn't there. The memory of his death, the smashing of the killing rock, the agony on his first friend's face, played itself out over and over again in Oog's mind. The thudding pendulum of sadness that was Oog's beating heart was growing a sharpened edge. The people who did this, who took Groog from him, these WeFolk, they must be made to suffer.

"Come," Em said, rising, and breaking Oog's train of thought. "We must go."

A short time later, Oog and the Townsfolk came within viewing distance of the entrance to The Village. They stayed hidden in the trees and watched.

"Are those the WeFolk?" Em whispered, pointing to a group of people with sticks and shields outside the wall.

"No," Oog answered.

"Are they The Village People?"

Oog looked closely. "No, I don't think so."

"Then who are they?"

Oog looked closer still. "Krog?"

"Who?"

"Krog," he said to Em, a broad smile on his face.

Oog stood up. "Krog!" he called out. Many of the Townsfolk crouched lower, aghast that Oog was revealing their position.

"It's okay," he told them, "it's okay! He's a friend."

64.

It had been a full day since Krog's army of the People Who Like Each Other and Trees had hurled rocks over the wall, and nothing had changed.

"Throw all the rocks we want," someone from the other side of the wall had yelled after the initial volley. "We're not coming out."

Krog ignored the strange use of grammar, shouting back, "We only want our friends to be released."

"If we give us up we've got no..." the voice paused for a moment, as if it was consulting someone else. "Leverage," it finished. "We've got no leverage."

Since then, silence.

Krog had shouted out and pleaded with the people on the other side of the wall. He had directed his comrades to make one more attempt at throwing rocks. Nothing worked and Krog was beside himself with worry. *What is going on in there?* he'd wondered. *Are Dag and Bilga okay? Were they hurt in our attack?* He would never forgive himself if they had been.

The people under his charge were growing restless, wanting him to either take action, or lead them away. But he couldn't just leave. He was running out of options and needed a bit of good luck.

Krog thought about luck, trying to sort out in his mind exactly what it was, and what caused it.

Luck, he thought, *is when a good thing happens at an unexpected but most welcome moment. Like meeting Oog.* He thought back on how he had first come to meet Oog.

Krog had been in his small cave during what the People of the Tree called "Reflection Time." He was supposed to be closing his eyes and thinking of trees. It was one of the rituals that had never made much sense to Krog. Couldn't he just go in the Forest and look at trees? Nevertheless, he tried each and every day, and each and every day he grew bored and his mind wandered.

On that particular day, he had been tossing three small pebbles in the air in a coordinated kind of dance. He had just hit his rhythm when Cagu called up to him. "Krog, I have someone I'd like you to meet." Krog followed Cagu to Oog's cave and his life was changed forever.

Maybe, he thought now, recalling that day, tossing pebbles makes luck. He looked on the ground, found three smallish stones, and began tossing them in the same synchronized dance. A few of his people saw what he was doing and came nearer, oohing and aaahing at his dexterity with the stones.

At that exact moment, Krog heard his name called loudly from somewhere off to the right. He dropped the stones and looked up just in time to see Oog step out of the trees. Oog called Krog's name a second time.

"Well, how about that?" Krog said aloud, mostly to himself. He went off beaming with delight at not only the reappearance of his relatively new but seemingly old friend, but in having discovered the source of luck.

Through either a highly improbable set of coincidences, or perhaps an unseen force in the universe, Krog would, throughout the remainder of his life, be able to summon good fortune simply by juggling stones. But that's a story for another time.

Oog and Krog embraced as the Townsfolk and the People Who Like Each Other and Trees mingled and did their best (the language barrier between some of them making it difficult) to get acquainted.

Oog told his story to Krog, including the murder of Groog by Tall Man. "Did you see Dag?" he asked.

"I did. Just before they closed the gate. She looked unharmed."

Oog nodded, relieved.

"So, what do we do now?" Krog asked.

Oog looked over his shoulder at his friends from Town. He understood their arguments about the danger of using fire, that he would be going down a path from which it would be difficult to retreat. But wasn't saving his friends the only thing that mattered?

Or was it?

Groog had once told Oog that ends do not justify means.

"I don't understand," Oog had said when Groog introduced the topic.

"What you do and how you do it matter just as much as what you're trying to achieve," Groog had explained.

"I still don't understand."

"Consider hunger."

"Okay," Oog had said, "I'm thinking about being hungry."

"Now, suppose you don't have any food, but Grag does."

"I will ask him to share it with me."

"Suppose Grag says no."

"I will forage for other food."

"You can't find any."

"I will leave the camp and go in search of food."

"You can't," Groog had said. "Your leg is broken."

Oog had looked at his leg. "My leg is fine."

"This is a hypothetical. Do you remember what that is?"

Oog did remember. Groog had taught him about hypotheticals only a few days earlier. Oog loved them. "So, I am hungry, Grag has the only food, he will not share it with me, and I cannot forage for more."

"Correct. What do you do?" Oog had no answer. "Do you just take the food?"

"Yes! I take the food. Grag can forage for more."

"Sorry," Groog had said, a mischievous smile showing at the corners of his mouth, "his leg is broken, too."

"Of course it is." Oog had been unable to contain his smile. "Okay, I give up."

"The point is," Groog had said, "even though your very real and necessary goal is to get the food, needing and wanting it is not enough of a reason to deprive Grag of the food. The ends, food, don't justify the means, stealing."

"So, I die?"

"No, you try harder to convince Grag to share."

"But what if he won't?"

"All we can do is try our best."

While Oog wasn't sure he understood the point of Groog's story, he still loved the logic puzzles his mentor shared with him. The memory of it now steeled Oog's resolve even more.

He had to free his friends, and, if he was being honest, he had to punish the people who had killed Groog. *These ends,* he thought to himself, *justify any and all means.*

"Oog?" Krog asked, and repeated his question. "What do we do now?"

Oog turned back to Krog, and said, "Fire. We use fire."

65.

When Oog fled The Village, No Name and Bob followed. No Name was certain Oog was the key to fire. But Oog had too big of a head start, and not only was he was fast, Bob was slow.

The two refugees tracked the young fire keeper for a while before the trail went cold. They stopped in the midst of an unknown part of the Forest.

"Where to now?" Bob was stooped over, hands on his knees, trying to catch his breath. As he had done so many times throughout his life, most recently with the WeFolk, Bob was surrendering his free will to that of another.

No Name sniffed the air and tried to use his power of thought.

Where should we go? We could keep following Oog, but any direction we choose to go from here would be nothing more than a guess.

No Name surveilled the woods around him. It was unfamiliar, but it wasn't inhospitable. Maybe he and Buh-ohb should leave all these strange thinkers behind. They could stay here and start a new life. He tried to imagine the two of them building a cave made from wood, tracking game, picking berries. It was a simple and beautiful daydream, and it was right there for the taking. No Name smiled.

"What?" Bob asked.

The question broke No Name's reverie, and he knew the dream could never come to pass, at least not yet. The plan was missing one critical element, something No Name's twisted soul could not leave behind: Fire. He simply had to have fire.

No Name turned to face his friend. "Buh-ohb, come."

The two retraced their steps, returning to the wall outside The Village. They stayed hidden in the trees as they watched the WeFolk guards return with Bilga, Cagu, and the Formerly-Great-and-Powerful-and-Now-Utterly-Banished Zook. They were amazed by the appearance of Krog and his army. And they were shocked and delighted at the return of Oog, now traveling with his own army.

No Name could make no sense of what was happening. When he tried to get Buh-ohb to use words to explain it, he found his friend was at a loss, too.

And then, Oog created fire.

NOTES ON MORALITY

Before people could think, they always did the right thing. Or rather, they never did the wrong thing. Or rather-rather, they just did things with no moral scale against which to judge them.

Eat some berries? Good on you.

Pick your nose? Hey, sometimes you just have to clean house.

Fornicate? Sure. Have fun.

It wasn't until the very first thinking person evaluated his actions against an invisible moral compass that things began to change.

Do these berries belong to someone else?

Why am I so self-conscious when my finger is up my nose?

Why will no one fornicate with me? Is it because I pick my nose?

Thinking and doing the right thing, it seemed, were intertwined. You couldn't have one without the other.

During the earliest days of thought, there were moral absolutes.

I should not kill other people.

I should not take what isn't mine.

Picking my nose is gross.

But as time wore on and societies became more complex, ideas that once seemed black and white faded to gray.

I shouldn't kill other people, but what if killing a person will stop them from killing someone else?

What if the thing I'm taking is of no use to the person who possesses it, but will save my life? For instance, a starving man stealing berries from a man with more food than he can use.

People shun me when I pick my nose, but aren't they secretly picking their noses, too?

At the end of the day, humans have their own counsel to guide them, and even then, only when they're prepared to listen to it. For that is the great crime of humanity: If we stop to think about it, we pretty much always know the right thing to do, but that doesn't mean we're going to do it.

66.

Oog and Krog worked together to fashion a very long stick. At Oog's direction, they found dead branches on the forest floor, stripped them of their smaller branches and leaves, and lashed what remained together with vines. They used more vines to tie small bundles of leaves and twigs to what would be the very top of the pole and laid it flat.

Oog went to work with his two rocks, banging them repeatedly, while Krog blew on the sparks as they landed on the kindling. In no time at all, there was a healthy blaze. Krog nodded with both amazement and appreciation. Together, the two friends lifted the pole and started toward the wall.

"Oog," Sica said, from behind him. "I beg you to consider what you're doing." Her tone was somber.

Krog looked from Oog to Sica and back again. "What's she talking about?"

"They don't want me to use the fire," Oog said. "But they're wrong. We must show our strength."

"Is there no other way to do that?" Sica asked.

"None as convincing as this," Oog said.

"Oog," Em began. She and the rest of the Townsfolk were standing beside Sica. "May I ask you one question first?"

Oog felt hemmed in, ambushed. He must use the fire before he lost his nerve. But these people were his friends; they deserved his attention. He gave a curt nod to Em.

"Can you control the fire?"

"Yes," he answered without even thinking, "I am a fire keeper."

"I see. Please explain then, before you go forward, what you plan to do with the fire."

"Their wall is made of wood. I will set fire to it, burning it down. They will be terrified, and we will free our friends."

"I see," Em said again. Her calm demeanor was making Oog more and more anxious. "And the caves inside the wall. What are they made of?"

"They are also made of wood," Oog answered, sensing the logical trap into which he was walking.

"And how do you know these will not also burn? How do you know you are not putting your friends in more jeopardy?"

Krog looked at his friend. "Oog? Is this true?"

"We must do something!" Oog was on the verge of losing all control of his emotions, but he didn't care. "These men, these WeFolk, they must pay for what they've done." Tears were streaming down his cheeks. "Groog..." But he couldn't finish the sentence.

Oog looked at Krog and Sica and Em. He looked at wizened old Aden and all the others. He looked up at the burning torch he had made.

And in that moment, his heart broke.

Oog realized—or maybe he was admitting what he'd known all along—his actions were about revenge, not justice. And while revenge may be a dish best served cold, it's better to leave it off the menu entirely.

Oog nodded. He would need to find another way.

But before he could lower the flaming pole and extinguish the fire, a bloodcurdling scream split the air in two.

67.

The scream was so loud it literally curdled the blood of a nearby Twizzlevarmint, causing it to fall out of the tree in which it had been protesting the tyranny of the queen. The Twizzlevarmint, whose name was Cesar, died on the spot.

At first, Oog thought the scream had come from the other side of the wall. But when a second scream came, he realized it was echoing off the wall, and that its source was behind him. And this second scream was much closer than the first.

Oog turned around just in time to see two men, both with red smeared on their faces, rushing toward him.

No Name, stronger and faster than Bob, was first to the scene. So startled were Oog and Krog that they let the pole fall. The top, the part with the burning bush, which was now a robust flame, fell directly onto the top of the wall, the burning leaves hanging over the edge.

No Name stormed past a very confused Oog and Krog, reaching the wall just as the flames leapt from the pole to the wood of the gate.

"Nooooo!" yelled Oog.

"Uh oh," muttered Krog.

Both watched as flames crackled down the outside of the wall, using the new fuel to grow at an exponential rate.

While No Name was a very smart thinker, he was also a very inexperienced thinker. So consumed was he with the need to possess fire, he leapt up in a wild attempt to grab the flames. He jumped three times before realizing he himself was on fire. Given that his body was covered with hair, he never had a chance. It was a painful death that no creature, not even one as pathetic and tragic as No Name, deserved.

No Name's short and sad life flashed before his eyes as he succumbed to the flames and smoke. He recognized his own folly and wished with all his heart he had made better choices. His final thought was so profound that, had he been able to communicate, it would have changed the entire course of human history. But that is a story for another time.

Bob skidded to a breathless stop next to Oog and Krog.

"Tried to...stop...him," Bob panted.

"What?" Krog was thoroughly confused. "This isn't a WeFolk attack?"

"No," Bob wheezed. "Just that one crazy little guy."

"What do we do?" Krog asked.

"We put out the fire," Oog answered.

"But how?" Bob and Krog asked in unison.

Oog didn't have an immediate answer, but he knew how to find one. "Now," he said, "we try our very hardest, all of us," he called over to the stunned Townsfolk, "to think."

68.

Inside The Village, Dag, Clint, Bilga, Cagu, and the Formerly-Great-and-Powerful-and-Now-Utterly-Banished Zook were all in the Holding House. They had been dragged there after Krog's first volley of rocks and had been there long enough to have lost track of time.

A guard had brought them food, and later, long after it had grown dark, five guards let them out one at a time to stretch and relieve themselves. Other than that, they were imprisoned.

Dag thought about making a run for it when it was her turn to go outside, but where would she go? The entrance gate was likely still closed, and trying to go over the wall seemed like a bad idea. She allowed the guards to return her to the confinement of the Holding House without protest.

The next morning, she was still trying to puzzle a way out of the prison when Bilga broke the silence. "Maybe we can tunnel our way out."

Dag didn't trust Bilga. He may have been in there with them, but he was, she had learned, the father of the idiot who had led the People Who Liked Other People but Didn't Seem to Like Her. It's a wonder, she thought, he isn't covered in green paint.

"Tun-nel?" Cagu asked, sounding out the strange word.

"It's a hole you dig in the ground to go under something." Bilga used hand motions to mimic digging. No one responded. "Really? C'mon, guys. A tun-nel."

"Tun-nel," Cagu said again.

"What's the purpose of this tunnel?" Clint asked.

"To get out of here," Bilga offered.

"Hey, good idea, dad," the Formerly-Great-and-Powerful-and-Now-Utterly-Banished Zook offered. "And just know, I really like you."

"Shut up," everyone, even Cagu, said in unison. It was the fourth time since they'd arrived that Zook had tried to like someone. The group had had enough.

At that precise moment, as they were collectively calling for the Formerly-Great-and-Powerful-and-Now-Utterly-Banished Zook to shut up, they heard a commotion coming from outside the Holding House. People were running and screaming, and one voice, louder than the rest, was yelling "Fire!" over and over again.

"Try the door," Bilga said.

"What," Zook answered, "you mean, like eat it?"

"No, you moron, try to open it."

"Oh. Right."

"Wait," Clint said. "Didn't we try that already?"

"I didn't," Dag answered.

"Me neither," offered Zook.

"Nor I," said Bilga.

"Aperire possumus ianuam?" Cagu said.

"Hey, I really like i-a-nu-am," Zook interjected, sounding out the unusual word.

"Shut up," came the communal response.

"Oh, for crying out loud." Dag walked over to the door, turned the handle, and pulled. To everyone's surprise, delight, and embarrassment, the door opened.

While the surprise was reaffirmed on seeing the scene outside the Holding House, the delight was short-lived. A tower of billowing smoke came from the direction of the front gate.

NOTES ON WATER

In the Heart of the Sea, you will find not only the Soul of an Octopus and a Fish Called Wanda, but also a Deep Calm. Yet, we Homo sapiens cannot live 20,000 Leagues Under the Sea. No. We can only Sit on the Dock of the Bay, cross a Bridge over Troubled Water, or embark on a Surfin' Safari, watching The Ocean Ripple as we pass.

"Take Me to the River," people say. "Rock Me on the Water."

"God Willing and the Creek Don't Rise," others answer.

But what does it mean?

It's nonsense, of course; a Perfect Storm—a Sharknado, if you will—of Sea and Sand, Purple Rain washing away the Smoke on the Water.

And yet, we terrestrial beings, landlubbers as it were, who exist not Under the Sea but On the Waterfront, fear the day When the Levee Breaks. For while We Are Water Protectors, we cannot live Life in a Fishbowl.

Boom.

In the meantime, supersaturated shenanigans aside, Oog was desperate to find a source of water to extinguish the fire. Luckily, he knew just the spot; the place where A River Runs Through It.

69.

Like most settlers, The Village People had chosen their plot of land based on its proximity to fresh water. A stream ran through the far northern end of The Village, entering underneath the western wall and leaving beneath the eastern. Oog hadn't seen the stream on his first trip to The Village; it was Aden who had found it when their group rested outside the wall just a few hours earlier.

Oog recalled the many lessons Groog had taught him about tending fire. The first and most important was that water ate fire. For the umpteenth time, he wished Groog was here.

"The stream," Oog said to Krog. "We need to get water from the stream to put out the fire." Oog was manic with worry about Dag. If the wooden caves on the other side of the wall were burning, he knew she would be in grave danger. And this was all his fault. If anything happened to Dag, he would never forgive himself. "We must hurry!"

"But how?" Krog asked. Not only was the stream two hundred paces away—Pythos, the former Person of the Tree obsessed with counting, had measured it and reported back to Krog when they first encountered The Village—none of them had a clue as to how to transport water.

It was Em, the very young leader of the Townsfolk, who hit on a brilliant idea.

Krog's army had brought shields. When held flat and turned upside down, each was, in essence, a large shallow bowl capable of holding water. Krog immediately saw how clever an idea this was. "Nero," he said, "fill your shield with water, carry it to the flames, and throw it on the fire."

Nero made a valiant attempt, though he took Krog's words too literally and threw the entire shield at the fire. But it wouldn't have mattered. The walk from the stream to the burning wall took far too long, and far too much water was spilled along the way.

Aden, the very wise elder, came to the rescue.

"If we space out evenly," he began, "between the stream and the fire—"

"The growing fire," interjected one of the People Who Liked Each Other and Trees.

"The growing fire," Aden continued. "It will only be six paces between each of us. We will move the water more quickly and drop less of it this way."

"How do you know how many paces there will be between us?" Oog asked.

"The GROWING fire," emphasized the same very anxious man.

"Something I invented called method metrics," Aden answered, a twinkle in his eye. "I will show you when we return home. It will blow your mind." (It is of note that over the millennia, the name method metrics would be shortened to mathematics, and would save many, many people from many, many things, and would blow many, many minds.)

With that, the group sprang into action.

They used two of their rank—Nero and Pythos—as runners, each taking empty shields from the front to the back of the line. Pythos counted each person in the line each time he passed until Krog asked him to stop.

Oog refined their process further by directing every third shield full of water to be thrown on the section of wall adjacent to the fire, to stop the flames from spreading.

Working in this way, they tamed the blaze and brought it under control.

70.

Every last one of The Village People was running away from the front gate. Cagu and the Formerly-Great-and-Powerful-and-Now-Utterly-Banished Zook joined their ranks. To Dag, that meant there was only one smart course of action.

"C'mon," she said to Clint as they emerged from the Holding House, taking a step in the direction of the smoke.

"What, toward the fire?"

"Yes."

"You do see everyone else running away from the fire?"

"Fools leading fools," Dag said. "Besides, I'm pretty sure the smoke means Oog is back."

Clint looked from Dag to the running people, back to Dag, and finally to the gate, which was no longer just a source of smoke, but was visibly on fire. "Sure," he said, "it's no dumber than anything else I've done in the last few days."

"I'm coming with you," Bilga said.

Dag shrugged and took off at a trot, Clint and Bilga staying close behind.

By the time they reached the gate, having made it through the throng of escaping The Village People and WeFolk, only Tall Man and A were left.

"Oooooog, we are an enemy of the people and we demand we

surrender ourselves. And we demand we turn off this fire!" Tall Man's shouts could barely be heard above the blaze.

"What's he talking about?" Bilga asked. "Who's 'we'?"

"What's happening?" Dag ignored Bilga and addressed her question to A.

"What's happening," he answered, "is that your boyfriend is trying to burn down my The Village."

"Oooog!" Tall Man bellowed.

"He can't hear you over the roar of this fire," Dag said. "I can barely hear you."

"So, what do we do now?" Clint asked.

"Do either of you know how to turn off a fire?" A interrupted.

"Wa—" Dag started to answer and stopped herself. "Yes," she said to A. And then she went silent.

"Well?" A demanded. "Time is wasting. Our whole The Village will be destroyed."

"And what will you give us in return?" Dag asked. "What's in it for me?"

Tall Man laughed at Dag's comment. "Clever. Do we see what we did there?"

A turned to Tall Man. He'd had enough. "It's not we. There is no collective we. You're a person same as the rest of us, you...you...you imbecile!"

Tall Man squared his shoulders and turned to face A. "What did we call us?"

"NOT US! YOU! YOU are an IMBECILE!" A was screaming now.

One of the logs from the gate broke and fell less than twenty feet from the two men, but neither one seemed to notice.

"We don't know this word, but we infer it is not very nice." Tall

Man's tone was cold and sharp. "Not surprising coming from a greed monger, a hoarder, an owner!" This last word was said with particular venom.

"Are these guys for real?" Bilga asked Clint in a whisper.

"Sadly, yes."

A's entire face turned red, and not just from the heat of the blaze. He exploded, his inner five-year-old having been awoken. "Imbecile! Imbecile! Imbecile!" And then he charged Tall Man, ramming his shoulder into his foe's midsection, and tackling him to the ground.

Just as the two men went down—A screaming "Imbecile, imbecile, imbecile!" over and over again—the rest of the gate collapsed, the flaming logs landing directly on the two adversaries.

Dag, Clint, and Bilga were standing too close. The three of them screamed in fright, jumping back and hitting the dirt. Dag was certain this was the end. Her final thought was for Oog, hoping he was somehow, somewhere safe, but fearing the worst. She closed her eyes and waited for the flames to swallow her.

71.

But the flames never reached Dag, Clint, and Bilga. The fire seemed to be more smoke than anything else now. It was retreating.

Using great caution, Dag stood up and surveyed the scene. Scattered logs, some still burning, more producing giant clouds of gray smoke; it was an image of total destruction. Her hair was singed, and she was coughing from the airborne ash.

Then, as if by some sort of magic, Oog and Krog walked through the clouds of billowing gray vapor.

Dag dropped to her knees, and her hands covered her mouth.

"I like what you've done with the place," Krog said, smiling. He put out a hand and helped Dag to her feet.

She choked a laugh and gave him a quick and strong hug. Then she turned to face Oog. "I thought you were dead."

"For a while, so did I."

"I'm sorry about Groog." Dag's voice was soft and gentle. She reached for his hand.

"Me, too," Oog muttered.

Dag's eyes were wet, but she was smiling. It was her smile that finally cracked Oog's armor. Everything from the last few days that had been pushed down to the deepest part of his being—the overwhelming anguish at the loss of his friend, the rage at those responsible, the dark path his soul had traveled, the incomprehensibility of it all—sprang to the surface, erupting like a volcano.

Oog cried.

Dag cried.

They both cried.

And then they cried some more.

NOTES ON THINKING, REDUX

I think, therefore I am," said Rene Descartes with confidence and ease to the room full of admirers. Now a seasoned and well-respected philosopher, he basked in their applause and their adoration.

A young, unknown philosopher—the same age Descartes had been when he attended his first meeting—waited for the tumult to die down, then asked a question. "But what if you're wrong?"

"But what if I'm right?" replied Descartes, clearly ready for the question. Again, applause.

"If you're right, you go right on existing," the young unknown philosopher began.

"Exactly. I'm here, therefore—"

"Yes, yes, therefore wherefore shmerefore," said the young unknown philosopher with no small amount of impatience.

Shmerefore? Descartes's hackles were up now. "Look. I'm here. I aaaaam." He drew this last word out to make his point. "You can see me, can't you?"

"I can."

"So that proves it."

"Proves what?"

"Proves that I am."

"It proves nothing?"

"Do you not trust your own eyes?"

"Have your eyes never deceived you?" the young unknown philosopher asked.

Descartes, known for his honesty, considered this question. "Well, there was this one time when I thought I saw Fermat across the road."

"And?"

"It turned out to be a mule." At this, the audience laughed, causing Descartes to blush. It had been many years since this audience had laughed at him. He was now one of their leaders and the humiliation stung. "It was a trick of the sun," he offered in his own defense.

"Or perhaps it betrays what you really think of Fermat," the young unknown philosopher said, getting another rise out of the audience. Sensing a turn in the tide, he plowed ahead before Descartes could protest. "Either way, it's proof your eyes cannot be trusted."

"Fine," snapped Descartes. "But you can hear me, can you not?"

"Actually, no, we're corresponding by written word. I cannot hear you at all. Now that I think about it, I can't really see you, either."

"What written word? What about this audience?"

"A construct to add flavor to the scene. A thought experiment, if you will."

"And if I will not?"

"You will not, so you are not?" Now the audience that didn't really exist was howling with delight.

"Ah," Descartes said, wagging a finger no one could see because he was, allegedly, communicating by written word. "But you are communicating with me. Therefore, I am."

"Wait. Are you now saying, 'You're talking to me, therefore I am?'" Descartes was silent. "Seems a little thin, doesn't it?"

"Thin or not," Descartes retorted, "it still proves my maxim. You communicating with me proves we are both here. If I'm here, communicating, then I am thinking. And if I think, I must therefore—"

"It doesn't prove we're both here," the young unknown philosopher interrupted.

"Oh, for the love of...what now?" Descartes narrowed his eyes, though again, there was no one there to see it.

"Well, suppose you're a figment of my imagination..."

"But I'm not!"

"Hmmm. That's exactly the kind of thing a figment of my imagination might say."

"This is preposterous."

"No, no, it's quite logical," the young unknown philosopher was growing excited. "I think of you, and therefore you are. If I don't think of you, you cease to exist."

"Prove it," Descartes snapped.

The young unknown philosopher turned his back on Descartes.

"Well," Descartes said, "I'm waiting."

Again, no answer.

"Ah, I see what you're doing," Descartes offered with a nervous smile. "If you don't acknowledge my existence, then I don't exist. But even if I don't exist to you, I still exist to myself. I know it to be true, because I can hear this dialogue in my head."

"Can you?" the young unknown philosopher asked, allowing himself to be drawn back into the conversation. "Suppose this entire conversation is taking place inside my head." He tapped his own skull. "Or even better, inside the head of an unseen, neutral third party."

"So, you're saying that because experience has taught me not to trust my external senses, and because any interaction I have with the world could actually be the result of someone else's internal monologue, I don't really exist?"

"Exactly," said the young unknown philosopher.

Descartes sat down on the ground and pondered this. The more he thought about it, the more circular was the journey of his mind. "I think I think, therefore I think I am?" he muttered to himself. "No, that doesn't work. Are you sure I don't exist?"

"Think about it."

Descartes did. A moment later, he vanished in a poof of tautological smoke.

"Well, that's a shame," said the young unknown philosopher. "I was just beginning to like him."

72.

Oog, Dag, Clint, and Em stood before the smoldering ruins of the gate to The Village. People around them were hauling burnt pieces of wood outside of the perimeter wall under Krog's direction, Bilga serving as an able lieutenant.

Dag motioned toward Krog. "He's a natural leader."

Oog had his arm around her shoulders, and she was leaning into his body. Physically, mentally, and emotionally exhausted, Oog could only nod.

"Hey, everyone," Krog called. "Over here."

Krog stood next to three of his workers, all of them looking down at a piece of parched earth. The splintered remains of a charred log had been recently moved to the side. Laying there, crushed and burned, was all that was left of A, leader of The Village People, and Tall Man, the leader of the WeFolk. Clint turned and vomited. Oog, Dag, and Em just stared.

"Who was that?" Em asked, her voice thick with sadness.

"It was A," Dag answered, "the leader of The Village People." She told the story of the final battle between A and Tall Man. The group fell silent for a moment. Finally, Em spoke.

"We should bring everyone here to see their remains."

"Why, Em?"

"See A?" she asked. "And the Tall Man? They stand as a monument to the folly of all people. We must learn from this."

Everyone was quiet for a moment, before returning to the work of removing burnt logs.

A handful of the people from each of the tribes—some of The Village People, some of the People Who Liked Each Other and Trees, and some of the WeFolk, though none of the Townsfolk—simply wandered out of the gate and into the Forest not to be seen again. This included both Cagu and the Formerly-Great-and-Powerful-and-Now-Utterly-Banished Zook. But more stayed and helped, and as the day wore on, the area around the gate became increasingly cleared of debris.

Under Krog's leadership, they were salvaging what they could and discarding the rest. By the end of the day, they had a plan for rebuilding the front gate. Bilga, Nero, and Buh-ohb—who was once again just Bob—had proved especially eager to help and were useful in organizing others. A new society was starting to take shape.

By early evening, Oog had made a roaring fire in a contained pit. Everyone, worn thin from the events of the past few days but buoyed by the camaraderie and community growing out of the effort to rebuild, gathered around the fire, told stories, laughed, and cried.

When the sun rose the next morning, Oog and Dag made ready to leave. They still needed to bring fire back to Mother's camp, and they needed to find Dag's home. Em, Sica, Aden, and the other Townsfolk also broke camp, ready to go back to their valley. The large group moved toward the gate.

"I wish you would stay," Krog said to Oog. "When we rebuild this place, we're going to send for the rest of our tribe. It's going to be the largest group anywhere in the Forest and we will very much need a fire keeper."

"Fire starter," Em corrected.

"Right," Krog smiled, "fire starter."

"I'm sorry, my friend," Oog answered, "we have promises to keep." He looked at Dag and then at his friends from Town. For the first time in his life, Oog felt the pull of a place. Dag nodded, and the two started to move again toward the gate.

"Clint?" Dag asked when she noticed her new friend lagging behind.

Clint was standing next to Krog, Bilga, and Bob. "I think maybe I've had enough adventure for a little while, and I think I can be of use here." The others all nodded.

Dag and Oog nodded, too. Each hugged Clint and Krog and followed the Townsfolk through the burnt gate and back into the Forest without saying another word.

73.

Do you know which way to go?" Dag asked.

Oog and Dag were at the fork in the road. They had said their goodbyes to the Townsfolk, once again promising Em and company they would come back to Town just as soon as they could; Em vowed to hold them to that promise and, with the others, began the walk back to their home.

Oog turned in a full circle, sniffing the air as he did. "No," he finally said in answer to Dag's question. "I'm not sure I do."

"Well," she said. "Behind us is The Village. That way," she pointed to where their friends could still be seen walking, "is Town. So, it's not in either of those directions."

Oog looked at her and smiled. Thinking really did have its benefits. He looked around again and this time something caught his attention. He couldn't say what. Perhaps the way the light played through the trees, perhaps a smell on the wind. Whatever the reason, he made his choice and they set off.

The couple walked for five days, sleeping beside a homegrown fire each night. On the sixth morning, Oog knew he was in familiar territory. He recognized boulders and bushes. Even the chattering of the Twizzlevarmint had the sound of home. Before the sun was at its peak in the sky, he wandered back into the camp of the People, his People.

He had been gone just three weeks, but it may as well have been three years. There were fewer people than when he left, and all looked bedraggled. No one rose to greet him; no one even seemed to notice that he and Dag had entered the camp.

Oog approached Mother, who was sitting on Groog's log deep in thought, and cleared his throat.

Startled, Mother looked up. "Oh, my goodness. Is it? Oog?" She was on her feet in an instant, wrapping him in an embrace.

"Mother," he said when she finally let go, "this is Dag."

Without words, Mother hugged Dag, too.

"Groog went after you," Mother said. "Did he find you?"

Oog hung his head, unable to find the words. He didn't need to.

Mother nodded as the tears streamed down her face. "I thought as much. That old fool. I told him not to go." Her tears turned to loud, wracking sobs. Others looked up and only now seemed to realize that young people were in their midst.

Grag walked up and looked Oog square in the eye. "Didn't even come back with fire, did you?"

Oog looked at his old fire pit and saw that Mother had prepared it. There was kindling piled on wood, the pit surrounded by clean stones. Oog smiled at Grag, knelt down, and used two rocks to make sparks. Within minutes, the fire was rekindled, and the camp was saved.

That night, a kind of memorial service was held for Groog. Everyone told stories, everyone laughed, and everyone cried. It was, to Oog's surprise, Grag who told the story of Oog's arrival in the camp, omitting no details. Dag was doubled over with laughter at the thought of Oog inspiring the words gilligan and genius in the same day.

When they were done remembering Groog—though Oog hoped he would never be done remembering his first and best friend—Oog and Dag told them about Town.

“Come with us,” Dag said. “There are young and old people together, and they have room to grow. It’s a wonderful place.”

No one volunteered, or stood, or even responded.

“But if you stay here...” Dag stopped herself from finishing the sentence, so Mother finished it for her.

“We’ll die. Yes, dear. But what better place to die than at one’s home?”

“I should stay,” Oog said.

“Nonsense,” Mother replied. “You should go. Squirrels leave the nest when it’s time, so too should our young.”

“But who will tend the fire?”

“Now that you’ve taught us how to create it, we’ll manage.”

There was nothing left to say.

The next morning, just after the sun rose, Oog left the camp for the second, and what he feared would be the last time.

“Are you sure you won’t come with us?”

“I’m sure,” Mother said, patting his wrist. “Leave this place now, but always carry it with you, here.” She tapped Oog’s heart.

Words failed Oog, so he hugged Mother again and took Dag’s arm. The young couple walked away without looking back.

74.

Oog and Dag didn't make directly for Town. They first needed to find Dag's home.

They left Mother's camp and walked in what they believed were concentric circles, always being careful to mark trees and keep their bearings. They went on like this for seven days, but nothing ever looked familiar to Dag.

"Maybe," she said at last, "I went further away than I realized."

"What would you like to do?" Oog asked.

Dag sat heavily on the ground and hugged her knees to her chest. "I don't know." Her voice was small, like a young child's.

Oog sat down next to her and held her hand. They stayed that way for what felt an eternity.

Dag leaned into Oog, feeling his warmth, taking in his scent, which was now so familiar, more familiar than any she could remember from her village. Maybe, she thought, home is where the heart is.

She squeezed his hand and made up her mind. "I think I'd like to go home now," she said.

"Of course," Oog said, "we will keep looking."

"No," she said, standing up, and pulling Oog with her. "Not that home."

Oog understood and hugged her.

Slowly, taking time to enjoy the Forest and everything in it, Oog and Dag made their way toward Town. They encountered many forms of life, saw beautiful sunrises dripping with fire, and spectacular sunsets in which the sky was awash with color. But they had no adventures, and they were glad of it.

When they finally reached Town, they were greeted by Em, Sica, and all of their friends. The Townsfolk had raised a roof in a small thicket of trees and had made the ground smooth. Sica had dug out a fire pit and surrounded it with small stones. This was to be Oog and Dag's new home. For the first time since each had set off on their adventures, the two lovers let the process of healing begin in earnest.

A week after Oog and Dag arrived back at Town, a bedraggled non-thinker wandered into the valley. It was Sica who found the young woman first. She was hungry and frightened and had to be coaxed from the stream into the heart of the village. She was given food, water, and most of all, affection.

When word of the newcomer's arrival reached Oog and Dag, they went to meet her. Oog didn't understand Dag's gasp at first, but when his one true love bolted forward and wrapped the newcomer in a tight embrace—an embrace which was returned in full force—and didn't let go, he knew this to be Girl, Dag's long-lost friend. Dag's eyes leaked with tears of joy for many, many hours.

As Oog, Dag, and Girl settled into the routine of life in Town, their days were filled with contentment and joy. You could almost say they lived happily ever after, but ever after is a very long time indeed.

NOTES ON ENDINGS

Beginnings beget endings. Or maybe endings beget beginnings. Or maybe middles are endings and beginnings with the important stuff lopped off.

The destruction of the Death Star, an ending, led to the creation of a new Death Star, a beginning. Walter White's ending is really just a new beginning for Jessie Pinkman. And the "beginning of a beautiful friendship" between Rick and Captain Renault might be the beginningest ending of all time. If art imitates life—and it does—then life, one might say, is just a ceaseless cycle of beginnings and endings.

With new horrors unleashed on the world, the innocence of life before this time in the Forest was forever lost. But humanity's greatest strength is its ability to adapt to change. How Oog and Dag would adapt to their ever-changing world, how their ending is really just a new beginning, is, of course, a story for another time.

LEN VLAHOS - AUTHOR

LEN VLAHOS is the author of several novels for teens and middle grade readers, including The Scar Boys, Life in a Fishbowl, and Hard Wired. Len dropped out of NYU film school in the 1980s to go on the road with his punk-pop band, Woofing Cookies (now available on major streaming services). Len has owned bookstores, worked behind the scenes in the book industry, and currently brings books and authors to large pop culture shows, including New York Comic Con. When he's not writing, you can find Len at the local hockey rink stinking up the ice, practicing and gigging with his #lamedadrock band -ish, or hanging with his wife, two sons, and menagerie of pets the Denver suburbs.

LEN VLAHOS-ACKNOWLEDGEMENTS

I've said it before and I'll say it again, while writing is a solitary process, publishing is collaborative. A large number of people helped shape this book from the moment the very first draft was finished, to the novel you've hopefully just finished reading. (Shame on you if you skipped ahead.) Editorially, thank you to beta readers Sandra Bond, Heather Duncan, Kristen Gilligan, Bobbi and Tom Gilligan, Jeff Hart, Alli Hellegers, Mark Lennertz, Amie Norris, and Sarah LaPolla. Your thoughtful feedback was instrumental in helping me better understand and craft the story. Thank you to Katelynn Tefft (bookseller extraordinaire) for giving the book an early read and providing such wonderful commentary. To Rich DiStefano for the wonderful illustrations. (Rich has been making me laugh since college, which was an embarrassingly long time ago.) To Kristen Gilligan for the wonderful cover. To Alli Hellegers for trying like hell (seriously, we were practically kicking in doors) to find a home for this weird little book with traditional publishers (tradpub, it turns out, doesn't really do "weird") and to Kristen Gilligan—yes, you're seeing her name a lot here —for being bold enough to publish it anyway. And to Kristen (yes, the same one), Charlie, and Luke, for giving me a really good reason to get out of bed every day. And finally, this book is something of an homage to Douglas Adams and all six members of Monty Python. My writing, my sense of humor, and on some level even my approach to life, were shaped by Arthur Dent, dead parrot sketches, Life of Brian, and so much more. I hope a whiff of a hint of a scintilla of that inspiration came across in this book.

RICHARD DISTEFANO - ILLUSTRATOR

RICHARD DISTEFANO has been a cartoonist in spirit, if not vocation, since the first grade. A graduate of Smithtown High School West (Long Island, NY) and New York University, he now lives and draws (and eats and sleeps) in southeastern Pennsylvania. He has two grown children. He sometimes tells people that he was the second man to walk on Neptune, but that may not be strictly true. The illustrations were created with a stylus pen using Adobe Fresco on a Microsoft Windows tablet. This approach offers clear advantages over traditional methods–for instance, an inked line can be much more easily erased or redrawn. On the other hand, when working with paper, the illustration doesn't suddenly vanish, only to be replaced by an error message!

RICHARD DISTEFANO - ACKNOWLEDGEMENTS

I would like to thank Len Vlahos for reaching back four decades into his past to invite me to illustrate this book. Thank you to Laura Scileppi for advising me on some of the business aspects involved in this project. Dani Bowman doesn't know me and I don't know her, but she made me realize that I don't need ink and paper to create illustrations. I probably would have eventually figured that out on my own, but she deserves my thanks anyway. My parents, Marianne and Joe, and my kids, Alex and Lindsey, had nothing to do with my work on this project. They deserve a mention here nonetheless. Finally, loving thanks to Diane. When an artist is his own worst critic, an enthusiastic and supportive partner can provide a valuable counterbalance. Thank you for being in a place where I could find you.

ABOUT THE PUBLISHER

LEFT FIELD PUBLISHING–where creativity meets collaboration. We're a forward-thinking publishing company created to combine the best attributes of traditional publishing with the best attributes of independent publishing. We exist to help authors bring their work to market in a cost-effective way while allowing them to retain control over their writing projects.

Our vision is to reimagine what publishing can be—bold, collaborative, and purpose-driven—by amplifying genre-defying voices across fiction, non-fiction, YA and kids books. Because great books aren't defined by a category.

Visit us at www.Left-Field-Publishing.com.

Connect with us!

Facebook: /leftfieldpublishing
Instagram: @leftfieldpublishing
TikTok: leftfieldpublishing
YouTube: @LeftFieldPublishing-m4g
LinkedIn: Left Field Publishing

www.ingramcontent.com/pod-product-compliance
Lightning Source LLC
Chambersburg PA
CBHW020841151025
34013CB00003B/8

* 9 7 8 1 9 6 6 8 8 3 0 0 5 *